Dark Horse

9

MUSTANG MOUNTAIN

Dark Horse

Sharon Siamon

Edited by Lori Burwash
Proofread by Elizabeth McLean
Cover photos by Michael E. Burch (mountains)
    and Douglas Kent Hall/ZUMA/Corbis, "The Cowboy Spirit" (horse)
Cover design by Roberta Batchelor
Interior design by Margaret Lee / Bamboo & Silk Design Inc.

Printed and bound in Canada.

Library and Archives Canada Cataloguing in Publication
Siamon, Sharon
    Dark horse / Sharon Siamon.

(Mustang Mountain)
ISBN 1-55285-720-4

    1. Horses—Juvenile fiction. I. Title. II. Series: Siamon, Sharon.
    Mustang Mountain.
PS8587.I225D37 2005   jC813'.54   C2005-902934-X

The publisher acknowledges the support of the Canada Council and
the Cultural Services Branch of the Government of British Columbia in
making this publication possible. Whitecap Books also acknowledges
the financial support of the Government of Canada through the Book
Publishing Industry Development Program for our publishing activities.

Please note: Some places mentioned in this book are fictitious
while others are not.

The inside pages of this book are 100% recycled, processed chlorine-free
paper with 40% post-consumer content. For more information, visit
Markets Initiative's website: www.oldgrowthfree.com.

To Bill

CONTENTS

Acknowledgments

I'd like to thank the following people for helping me research and write *Dark Horse*:

As always, Lori Burwash for her careful and insightful edit.

Dr. Wayne Burwash, equine veterinarian, for his expert knowledge of horses and their injuries.

Dr. Stan Alkemade, endurance race veterinarian, and his wife, Barbara, for sharing their experience of the world of international endurance racing.

Elaine and Rick Steele and their family, for making us welcome at endurance rides in eastern Ontario.

And special thanks to Marion Shearer for reading the manuscript with an endurance rider's eye.

CHAPTER 1

LOOSE HORSE

Becky woke up with something sharp sticking into her back. It was pitch dark. As she felt around, her hand hit cold metal above her head. Of course! Becky thought. I'm sleeping in a horse trailer.

She hugged herself with excitement. They were at the famous Wildflower 50 endurance race—camped in a grassy field with a lot of other horse trailers. Outside, in a tent, was her friend Rob Kelly. Her paint mustang, Shadow, was tied to a picket line near the trailer. Windy, her mother's chestnut mare, was in a pen next to the truck.

Tomorrow, whether it rained or snowed or the sun shone, she, fifteen-year-old Becky Sandersen, would climb into Windy's saddle and set off on a fifty-mile race that would take her high over steep mountain trails.

Becky shivered. It was cold in the trailer on this early September night. Was it the cold that had wakened her? Becky brushed her blond curls out of her eyes and stared into the darkness. She could hear her mom softly breathing in the bunk by her side.

A sudden noise made her sit up with a jerk and strike her head on the roof. What was that? Hoofbeats thudding on the grass?

A horse—running. Shadow? Windy?

Becky shook her mother's shoulder. "Mom!" she bellowed. "Wake up! There's a horse loose. If Windy's running free, we could lose the race! She could get hurt, or …"

A beam of light snapped on. Laurie Sandersen stared into her daughter's startled brown eyes.

"It can't be Windy," Laurie muttered, "unless you forgot to turn on the electricity in her pen."

"No, I didn't forget." Becky fumbled under the bunk for her jeans. The living quarters in the front of the horse trailer were packed tight with equipment for the race, a jumble of horse gear, riding equipment, food for the three of them and feed for the horses.

Becky found her jeans and quickly shrugged them on. Pushing open the trailer door, she switched on an outdoor light.

"It's okay, Mom," she called softly back to her mother. "Windy's here, but something's spooked her."

In the beam of light, Windy gleamed reddish gold in a corner of the pen—head up, tail up, every muscle ready for flight.

Becky glanced quickly at the picket line to make sure Shadow was still securely tied, then rolled her slight body under the electrified cloth-tape fence that enclosed Windy. She moved to the mare's side and stroked her quivering neck. "You're all right. What's out there?"

"What's up?" came a sleepy voice from the tent. The door unzipped and Rob unfolded his lanky frame from the tiny tent.

"We don't know—I heard a horse running, but Windy's okay," Becky said breathlessly.

At that moment, a tall girl in a white track suit came striding out of the shadows. "It's my horse, Hawk. He got loose. Help me catch him."

"Tara?" Becky gasped. She had met Tara Kosaric that evening, when she and her mother rolled in with a fancy trailer behind their big SUV. In the trailer was Tara's horse, Hawk. He was a beautiful dark gray Arabian with intelligent brown eyes and a twitchy disposition.

Tara had made herself instantly unpopular by arriving late and driving through the middle of the vet check area. By the time she set up, she was late for the ride talk. Then she'd insisted that all the rules and the route of the Wildflower 50 race be explained again, for her!

People had thrown disapproving glances at the willowy blond and her mother. Eva Kosaric was dressed in a long flowing skirt and large hat. She spoke with a strong accent, smiled at everyone and seemed to have no idea what she was doing at an endurance race.

But Tara did. "I'm so glad I'm not the only *young* person

in this race," she announced to Becky, with a scornful glance at the mostly middle-aged riders. "Hawk and I are going places. Once we win all the races around here, we'll enter the Tevis Cup, the biggest race in North America—maybe even race across the deserts of Arabia. Hawk can do it. He's one hundred percent pure Arabian."

Becky was about to tell her that she was riding the Wildflower 50 only because her mother had a sore back, but it was too late. Tara had spotted Rob.

The girl's gray-blue eyes had gleamed at the sight of Rob's fair hair and six-foot-three frame. "Is he your boyfriend?" she'd demanded to know. "I love tall guys. How old is he?"

"Rob's sixteen and he's just my friend. He's crewing for me tomorrow." Becky hoped with all her heart that Rob Kelly was much more than a friend, but she wasn't about to get personal with a girl she'd met half an hour before.

"Oh, that's *fantastic*—he's the same age as me!" Within ten minutes, Tara had talked Rob into helping her move her rig to a spot beside theirs.

"Maybe you could crew for me in the race tomorrow, too?" She'd looked up at him through a fringe of carefully curled eyelashes.

"Yeah ... maybe," Rob had stammered.

He seemed totally paralyzed by Tara, tongue-tied and fumbly. Becky suspected it had something to do with the fact that Tara looked like a fashion doll, with her long legs and ash-blond hair. Her eyes were a beautiful almond shape, her cheekbones were high, and her pony-tail fell gracefully over one shoulder. Side by side, she and Rob looked like matching blond bookends.

At this moment, Tara was even more appealing, with her hair loose around her shoulders. "Please help me find Hawk," she begged. "He's out there, all alone in the dark. What if he hurts himself?"

"I wonder how he got loose?" Laurie mumbled sleepily as she stepped out of the trailer. Hawk had been in a tape pen adjoining Windy's. Now the tape was broken, straggling across the grass.

"I don't know—maybe somebody let him out," Tara gasped.

"Who would do that?" Becky asked doubtfully.

"Oh, I have enemies at this race," Tara said in a low, dramatic voice. "They don't want Hawk to win."

"Endurance racing isn't like that." Becky rolled her eyes. "Nobody's out to hurt anybody else."

Tara flung her arms wide. "Don't be so naive. There are things about this race you don't know!"

"Did you have the electricity switched on in Hawk's pen?" Rob asked sensibly.

"No, Hawk doesn't need that electric current—at least, he never has before," said Tara haughtily. "I hate the idea of him getting shocks."

Becky snorted with disgust. As if a little piece of cloth tape was going to contain an excited horse. Hawk must have charged right through.

Just then, Windy lifted her head and gave a loud whinny.

They heard hoofbeats and then an answering whinny not far off.

"That's Hawk!" Tara squealed. "Let's go!" She started to dart into the shadows.

"Wait," Rob warned. "Chasing him will just make him run. Stay there. Maybe he'll come back to Windy—they seem to have made friends."

"If those two horses have bonded, I'll probably be riding the whole race with that blond troublemaker right beside me," Becky muttered to her mother.

Laurie put her arm around Becky's shoulder. "Well, it would make sense. It'll be easier for us to crew for you and Tara if you're together."

"Agggh," Becky groaned. "Is that supposed to be a good thing? I don't want you and Rob to crew for Tara."

"Endurance racing is all about helping one another." Laurie gave her a squeeze. "You'll find that out tomorrow."

"But, Mom, Tara's so crazy!" Becky hissed in her mother's ear. "This stuff about enemies…"

A soft whinny came from nearby. "Shh! Here comes Hawk," whispered Laurie.

"*There* you are, you bad horse." Tara's white-suited figure strode into the darkness and came back leading Hawk by the halter. In the light from the trailer, his dark gray coat looked even darker. The brown markings that dappled it looked like the hawks that soared over the mountain slopes.

Tara stroked his shoulder. "Rascal horse," she cooed. "Why did you run away like that?"

"Maybe he was thirsty." Rob pointed to an empty water bucket. "I'll get him some water. Then we'd better hook up the electricity to your fence so he doesn't escape again."

"I'll get water for Hawk and repair his pen," Laurie offered. "You three should get some sleep. You need to be rested for the race tomorrow."

"You are so *nice*, Mrs. Sandersen." Tara beamed. She turned to Rob. "And you're a lifesaver. You knew just what to do."

"It was nothing…" Rob smiled awkwardly—the shy smile he usually saved for Becky. She felt a sudden sting in her heart.

Laurie steered her toward the trailer. "Go on," she urged. "Back to bed."

Tara handed Hawk to Laurie. "Thanks, I really appreciate this." She tossed the words carelessly over her shoulder as she headed for her own trailer.

She has no idea of the trouble she's causing, Becky thought. She went to soothe Shadow, who was pacing back and forth on her picket line.

"Settle, girl." She stroked Shadow's brown and white hide. "The excitement's over, for tonight."

Rob's face poked out of the doorway of his tent as she passed.

"Don't worry." He smiled his shy smile at Becky. "Everything's going to be fine."

"Sure, Rob," she muttered. "Good night."

Fine? That's all he could say? Typical Rob! He was an amazing horse trainer and cowhand—he could do so many things—why couldn't he just say how he felt instead of telling her not to worry? They'd been together all summer at Mustang Mountain and not one word of love, or affection, or anything except small talk about horses and the weather. She'd had to beg him to come and crew for her at the Wildflower 50. But he'd jumped at the chance to crew for Tara, whom he'd just met!

Maybe he doesn't even *like* me that way, she groaned to herself as she turned away from Rob's tent and let herself into the trailer. Maybe it takes someone like Tara—tall, blond and gorgeous—to turn him on.

CHAPTER 2

THE WILDFLOWER 50

Back in her narrow bunk, Becky tried to shake off the sting of seeing Rob smile at Tara. She'd felt jealous before, when her cousin Alison had flirted with Rob. Becky knew how that first sliver of jealousy could grow into a green dragon that took over your entire life. How was she ever going to concentrate on the race tomorrow?

Becky punched her pillow in misery. I'm not even supposed to be racing, she thought. Windy is Mom's horse. *She's* supposed to be riding the Wildflower 50. *I'm* supposed to be crewing for *her*.

Her mind sped back to three days earlier, when all their plans had suddenly burst like a soap bubble.

Becky and Rob had been cleaning stalls in the barn at Mustang Mountain Ranch, where Becky lived and Rob was working for the summer.

Rob had stopped shoveling straw and manure into a wheelbarrow. "I need to talk to you, Becky."

When she looked up at him in surprise, she could see he had something important to say. Was this it? Was he finally going to tell her he was crazy about her? Maybe drop the stupid shovel, take her in his arms and kiss her?

"I—I have some bad news." Rob stumbled over his words, then finally blurted out, "I can't stay and help you crew for the Wildflower 50 this weekend. I have to go home, for school."

Becky stared blankly at him. *This* was what he had to say? That he was abandoning her on the most important weekend of her life? She brushed back her sun-streaked hair with an impatient hand. "You *could* stay one more weekend—if you wanted to," she begged. "School doesn't start until Tuesday."

Rob sighed. "Sara has to leave for vet college next week. She wants me home."

It was on the tip of Becky's tongue to say "You always do what your bossy big sister wants." But that wouldn't have been fair. Rob and Sara's parents had died a few years before, and the two were on their own. Becky knew they were pretty tight, even though Rob sometimes got tired of Sara always telling him what to do.

She went back to raking straw out of the stall.

"I just thought it would be nice if you were there to

help me crew Windy's first big endurance race," Becky gulped, "and … and I really want you to come."

She could feel her cheeks flush, but if Rob wasn't going to say anything, maybe it was up to her to tell him how she felt. "Rob, this whole summer, we've—I …"

"I love you," she wanted to say, but the words wouldn't come out. Instead, she pleaded, "Please, please stay—it's just one more weekend. When you're gone, it will be just Mom and Dad and me at Mustang Mountain for the whole winter. I'm going to miss you so much."

Rob cleared his throat. "Uh … I guess it will be kind of lonely staying up here. Why don't you come and live with Alison in Horner Creek and go to school near me? Or go and stay with your friend Meg in New York, like you did before?"

Becky whirled to face him. Not *one single word* about him missing her! She wanted to throw dirty straw in his face. Instead, she burst out, "It was a nightmare living with Alison. And I'd never go back to that snob school in New York. They treated me like some hick kid. Anyway, I *have* to stay. Dad's short-handed with you leaving!"

Her mother's call broke into her furious flood of words. "Hey, you two. I'm taking Windy for one last lope up the meadow before it gets too dark."

Becky glanced at her mother, saddling Windy in the crossties. Had her mother overheard them? She hoped not. Mom wouldn't like her begging Rob to stay for the Wildflower 50. She thought they could manage on their own—with her riding Windy, and Becky crewing.

Laurie headed out the barn door, leading the chestnut mare.

Becky shook her head. "I wish Mom wouldn't train so hard. Her back injury still bothers her."

"Don't worry," Rob said as they finished mucking out the stall. "Your dad will be at the race to look after her."

"No, he won't." Becky glared up at him. "There's a government inspector coming and Dad can't leave the ranch. I'm going to have to crew by myself."

"I'm sorry." Rob's blue eyes narrowed with concern. "You know I'd like to help, but I promised Sara I'd be home tomorrow night."

"Sure, I know." But Becky wondered how she'd manage to crew a fifty-mile endurance race alone. How could she get equipment, feed and water to the vet checks along the race course when she couldn't drive a truck? She supposed she could hitch rides with other crews, but it would be so much easier if Rob was there to drive.

As they walked out of the barn, Becky watched her mom ride Windy into the small creek that ran between the ranch and the mountain meadow. Shadows were creeping down the mountainsides, the setting sun turning the creek to gold. The water splashed up around Windy's knees.

Suddenly the mare lurched sideways, slipping on the wet rocks. Laurie fell, landing awkwardly in the fast-flowing stream.

Becky flew across the yard with Rob at her side. Windy was standing calmly on the far bank of the creek, her reins dangling. But Laurie was crouched in the middle of the stream, soaked.

"Danged slippery rocks—my back again—wouldn't you know!" She reached for Windy's reins and winced with pain.

"Here, Mom, we'll help you." Becky splashed into the shallow creek. Rob sloshed beside her. In two long strides, he had crossed the creek and gathered Windy's reins.

The mare tossed her head as if to say, "It wasn't my fault."

"If only I'd had the sense to quit." Laurie limped to shore, leaning heavily on Becky. "I've ridden across that creek a thousand times and never had this happen—I just wasn't balanced right."

Becky could see the lines of worry deepen beside her mother's mouth. "Windy's done so well. She deserves to go on this race."

"You're not thinking of pulling out of the Wildflower!"

"Let's get up to the house," her mom groaned. "I'll do some stretches on the floor and see what the damage is."

Waiting to find out how badly her mother was hurt, Becky and Rob shared the big leather couch in the Mustang Mountain Ranch living room.

"Mom has her heart set on this race," Becky sighed. "She did well in a couple of competitive trail rides and that local endurance race three weeks ago. They're ready for the Wildflower, even though Windy would be a real long shot to win."

"You've done a great job helping to train Windy." Rob rested his long arm on the back of the couch—for a moment Becky was sure he'd let it fall across her shoulders. "I'm proud of you—the girl who used to be scared of horses."

"You helped me get over being scared. You helped me train Windy, and Shadow when she was a wild mustang." Becky longed to grab Rob's arm and pull it around her. Why didn't he just hug her? she wondered miserably.

Rob had been an important person in her life since they'd met in Horner Creek earlier that year. When he got the summer job at Mustang Mountain, she'd been sure it was going to be the perfect summer. She and Rob—working hard, sharing adventures, getting closer every day.

But now it was September. Summer was over. And the best Rob could say was that he was *proud* of her? He sounded like a big brother, not a boyfriend!

At that moment, her mother limped to the living room door, supported by Becky's father, Dan. She was a small woman and looked even shorter bent over with pain.

"It's no use." Laurie shook her head. "We'll have to scratch the race—wait till next year."

The disappointment hurts worse than her back, Becky thought. They couldn't pull out of the race after so much hard work! She jumped to her feet. "Mom, let me ride Windy for you."

"I don't know, darlin'." Her mom shook her head again. "You haven't ridden a race before. And this is a tough one, even for experienced riders."

"I can do it," Becky insisted. "Next year I want to ride Shadow in endurance races—why don't I get some experience now?" This summer, her mustang, Shadow, had proved she had the makings of a great endurance horse, but her training had just begun.

Laurie raised one eyebrow. "Even if you could ride the race, honey, you don't have a crew. Rob has to go, and I couldn't lift a bucket." She glanced up at Becky's father. "And Dan's got to stay and meet the inspector."

There was a moment of disappointed silence.

Then Rob cleared his throat and stood up. "Uh... listen. I'll call my sister. Maybe she can spare me for Saturday, at least."

Laurie's face brightened like the sky after a storm. "Rob, that would be fabulous. If you can crew, maybe Becky *could* ride for me. You know what to do, you've been helpin' with Windy's training."

"I don't know," Dan broke in. "Like you said, Laurie, Becky hasn't ridden in a race before. And that's tough country, up where they hold the Wildflower 50 ..."

"She rode Shadow all the way from Rainbow Valley to get help for her friends six weeks ago," Laurie argued. "And she's been helping me train Windy all summer."

"But just Becky and Rob on their own?" Dan looked at the two of them and stroked his long mustache doubtfully.

Rob gave Becky an embarrassed glance. The tips of his ears turned pink.

"Oh—" Laurie poked Dan's arm, "you old stuffed shirt. I feel well enough to go along and chaperone— if that's what you're worried about." She laughed. "You go ahead and phone home, Rob. Let's hope Sara can spare you."

Becky crossed her fingers that Sara would say yes. While Rob went to use the radio-phone in the office, she dashed outside—crossed the dark yard to the paddock, slipped through the rails and took Shadow's soft muzzle in her hands.

"Wouldn't it be great," she whispered, "if I got to ride Windy in the Wildflower 50? We'd take you, to give you practice getting trailered and tied up with a lot of strange horses close by."

Becky often talked to Shadow at times like this, when her feelings were so strong she didn't want to show them to anyone else. "If only Rob *could* come!" she whispered fiercely as she stroked the little paint's velvety nose. "We'd all be there together. Maybe something would finally happen between Rob and me!"

Now Rob was here, and in a few hours the race would start.

I've got everything I wished for, so why am I so miserable? Becky asked herself, tossing and turning in her bunk.

If only that idiot Tara had looked after Hawk properly, we'd all be sleeping now.

"I wish Meg was here," Becky moaned into her pillow. Her best friend, Meg, would tell her she was being silly. She'd say that Rob was loyal and would never be swayed by Tara's long legs and candy-apple smile. But Meg lived on the other side of the continent.

If only her parents didn't live in such an isolated place. It was going to be so lonely at Mustang Mountain with nobody else around. Their ranch, high in the Rockies, was a great place to raise horses for mountain park patrol—not so great for a teenager whose nearest high school was three hours away by horseback and car. She'd have to finish school by correspondence.

"I can't think about that now!" Becky groaned softly. "I have to think about the race, the race, the race..."

"Becky?" came her mother's drowsy voice from beside her. "Are you okay?"

"Can't sleep."

"Don't worry, darlin'. You'll do just fine tomorrow. Trust me."

Becky reached out in the darkness and found her mother's hand—held it as if she were a little girl. She heard Windy and Hawk, snorting and blowing to each other in horse language, and Shadow, munching hay from her hay net. Finally, she fell asleep.

In his tiny pup tent, Rob squirmed uncomfortably, thinking about Tara. He'd never met a girl like her. You just said yes to whatever she wanted before you knew what you were doing!

Becky didn't like the idea of him crewing for Tara, he could tell. He hoped it wouldn't spoil the race for them.

Why hadn't he just said no? Rob kicked angrily at the twisted end of his sleeping bag. Because Tara had no one else to help her? Because he was a nice guy? Who was he kidding? It was because she was so amazing to look at.

Beside Tara, Becky seemed to pale. She was like a mountain wildflower, small and fine, while Tara... Tara was a long-stemmed rose that you couldn't take your eyes off because you couldn't believe anything could be so perfect.

Rob squirmed again. Becky's laughing face had turned so sour when Tara showed up. Becky's face—her bright eyes and rosy cheeks. Her wild curly hair. Her quick, sure way of walking. All summer he'd been wondering how to tell her what he felt—how he hoped she felt the same way. But now... with Tara... everything was mixed up.

Tomorrow he'd try to straighten it out.

CHAPTER 3

RACE DAY

The sun had risen as Becky and the other riders went through their race preparations. It lit the snowy peaks first, then crept down into the meadow, baking the trampled grass in Windy's pen.

"Remember to give Windy electrolytes at every rest stop." Laurie handed Becky doses of white powder the next morning. "It will help her drink more and keep her from getting too fatigued. I'll give her a dose now."

"She hates the stuff," Becky protested, stuffing the small plastic bags in her saddle bag.

"Maybe, but she'll need it. It's going to be a hot day." Laurie mixed the white powder with water and filled a large syringe. Like a human runner's power drink, the mixture provided valuable salts Windy would lose running hard.

She held the chestnut mare's glossy head high while she shoved the syringe into the corner of her mouth. Pressing on the plunger, she forced the milky liquid down Windy's throat.

Becky's legs felt sore and tight after a night in the cramped trailer bunk. She was dizzy from lack of sleep and sick with excitement. The sight of the electrolytes drooling out of Windy's mouth turned her completely off food.

Laurie frowned as she watched Becky refuse breakfast.

"I don't have to tell you how important it is to eat and drink enough on the trail," she warned. "When you get to the vet checks, you'll be so busy worrying about Windy that you're liable to forget to take care of yourself. Don't let that happen."

Becky nodded. "We've been over this, Mom."

Laurie went on, "Rob's your crew. Let him take care of Windy."

Becky glanced over to where Rob was helping Tara adjust her padded endurance saddle.

"Looks like Rob's going to be busy," she grumbled.

"Listen, Becky—" her mother grabbed her shoulder and turned her so they were eye to eye, "you can't let your feelings about Tara get in your way ... do you hear me? If you're jealous and angry, Windy will feel it and it will slow her down. Anything you're feelin' will affect her performance. If you're mad, or tired or depressed, she will be, too."

"I know, Mom." Becky shook off her mother's grip. "It's just that—"

"Stay positive!" Laurie insisted. "Otherwise, I might as well ride Windy with my sore back. The result will be the same."

"I hear you." Becky threw back her shoulders. "I can't waste all our hard work because of some gorgeous girl on a knockout horse!"

"And you'll have to watch Hawk," Laurie continued. "He's a knockout horse, all right, but I don't think he's properly trained for this event. My guess is he'll likely dash ahead at the start and tire quickly. Windy shouldn't keep up with him, but she might try. Look at them—it was love at first sight."

Hawk was nose to nose with Windy over the cloth tape that separated their pens. But while Windy was calm and composed, Hawk strutted and stamped as Tara and Rob tried to adjust his bridle. It was as if he couldn't wait for the race to start.

"Typical Arabian," Becky sighed. Most horses that won the big endurance races, especially the hundred-mile races, were purebred Arabians. They cooled off fast, which meant their heart rate quickly returned to normal.

She hoisted Windy's saddle into place. She knew her mom wanted her to ride Windy at a slow and steady pace. This race was for conditioning, not winning. But wouldn't it be wonderful, Becky thought with a shiver, if Windy had a chance at the ribbons?

She arranged Windy's carefully braided mane. "You could be the dark horse in this race," Becky whispered. "You know, the one that comes from behind and beats all the other horses? The one they least expect to win. Even though this is your first big race, you've got the stamina and heart to do it."

If only I can stay focused, and nothing slows us down, she added fiercely to herself.

The sight of a vet approaching with her clipboard broke Becky's concentration. Had they forgotten something in the vet check earlier?

Dr. Janet Harris was a young woman with a firm stride and sharp eyes. She passed Windy and walked over to Rob and Tara.

Becky couldn't help overhearing.

"Someone reported that your horse tried to kick his horse in line for the vet check," Janet said. "Do you want to tell me about that?"

"Hawk is just excited." Tara's wide mouth turned down at the corners. "That's all."

The vet pulled a red ribbon out of her jacket pocket. "Tie this around his tail," she said. "It's not a substitute for good manners, but it will warn other riders that your horse kicks and to stay away."

"All right." Tara took the ribbon. "But there's nothing wrong with Hawk."

"Nothing that good training won't fix." Janet looked sternly at the fidgety gray horse as Tara tied the red ribbon around his tail. "Remember that he can win the race on time, but lose it if he doesn't pass the vet check. This sport is all about looking after your horse."

Tara bit her bottom lip. "I can look after Hawk."

"Okay … it's just some friendly advice. Have you got electrolytes for him?"

Tara shrugged. "The best money can buy. I'll start giving them to him now."

"The most expensive isn't always the best." Janet shook her head. "Can I see what you're giving him?"

"Sure, it's here, in my trailer." Tara opened the back door.

Just then Tara's mother, Eva, peered out the window of the large trailer. "Oh! A nice red ribbon for Hawk's tail," she crooned. "Doesn't he look handsome?"

Janet turned to hide a smile. The red ribbon was no decoration. She took the container of electrolytes Tara handed her and quickly glanced over the ingredients. "I hope you haven't been giving him this!"

Tara looked stunned. "No, not yet, why?"

"This stuff could kill an endurance horse." Janet thrust it at her. "It's for race horses who do short sprints, not long distance. The mix of salts is all wrong."

"Oh—" Tara faltered. "Then I guess I won't use it."

"Be sure you don't. I'm sure some of the other riders would share their electrolytes with you. I'll ask around if you like."

"No, that's okay." Tara turned away with a haughty shrug.

Janet strode over to Becky and Laurie. "Good morning," she greeted them, reaching out to stroke Windy's muzzle. "Sorry to hear about your back, Laurie. How are you feeling?"

Laurie sighed. "Not well enough to sit on a horse for six hours or more."

"How about you?" Janet's challenging brown eyes met Becky's. "Are you ready to ride your mom's horse fifty miles? That's eighty kilometers, you know. And it's a tough trail."

"I think so." Becky gulped.

"She'll be fine," Laurie promised.

"Well, I'm glad you and Rob are crewing for Tara Kosaric." Janet sighed. "You'll be able to keep an eye on her—and she'll need to borrow some electrolytes, if that's okay."

"Sure," Laurie smiled. "Glad to help."

Janet gave them a quick wave and moved on to the next competitors.

Becky's heart sank. More links in the chain that tied her to Tara. If I have anything to do with it, she thought fiercely, Windy and I won't be anywhere near her and Hawk in this race.

Just then, there was a cry of dismay from Tara. "Look! They've wrecked my riding helmet. The beasts, I hate them."

"Oh, for Pete's sake," Becky groaned. "What now?" She turned to see Tara holding a crushed green endurance helmet by the strap, stomping toward them. Rob trailed behind her.

"I found it, squashed, behind my trailer," Tara announced. "The Belmonts did this, I'm sure. And I'm sure they were the ones who let Hawk out last night, too."

"Who are the Belmonts?" Becky, Laurie and Rob asked together, staring at Tara and her ruined helmet.

CHAPTER 4

Fast Start

"That woman, over there." Tara pointed to a gray-haired woman with a sharp face, doing up her own helmet. "That's Gwendolyn Belmont, my enemy. And that man—" she pointed to a slim older man in black tights and a black T-shirt, "is her brother Graham Belmont." Her voice dripped scorn. "I call them the Gee-Gees."

"What makes you think they ruined your helmet?" Laurie took it from her hand. "It looks as though someone drove over it—could have been an accident."

"There are no accidents where the Belmonts are concerned," Tara muttered darkly, "and there are things about this Wildflower race you don't know."

"Don't be so dramatic," Becky scoffed. "What is this big mystery?"

"You'll find out, when the race is over and Hawk and I have won." Tara tossed her head.

"Well, you're not going to win anything unless you get your horses warmed up and ready for the start," Laurie pointed out. "Becky can lend you a helmet, Tara. Your heads are about the same size."

"Except mine isn't swelled," Becky groaned to herself. She stalked off to the trailer to find a helmet for Tara. Her mom always insisted on bringing two of everything in case of emergency. Obviously, Tara didn't bother with details like that.

"Windy, take it easy. This is just the warm-up, not the race!"

Mounted on Windy, Becky studied the other twenty-five horses. Grays of all shades, blacks, chestnuts and bays, they glowed with health and eagerness to race. The two vets had checked their pulse and respiration rates. Every detail of each horse's condition was noted on a ride card. Becky's was safely stowed in a plastic sleeve in her saddlebag.

Windy had passed the vet check with flying colors. Janet had smiled as she filled out the mare's card. "She's in top condition. Congratulations."

Hawk, Tara's horse, hadn't done so well. Despite looking like a champion, his muscle tone was not as good as Windy's. Watching him prance and skitter around the start area, Becky wondered whether his superb Arabian breeding would make up for the training he hadn't had.

Tara didn't act like she was worried. She let Hawk trot in wide circles. The red ribbon tied to his tail kept the other riders out of his way. Hawk was like a bully with a big stick cutting across a playground full of kids. Nobody wanted to risk their horse getting kicked—it could put them out of the race, or worse.

Rob came striding toward Becky, the ride map fluttering in his hand. Becky slid from Windy's saddle to stand near him as he pointed out the first vet stop. "I'll meet you here." He pointed to an X he'd made on the map. "Your mom says she's going to stay at the trailer."

"Is she all right?" Becky felt a spasm of fear.

Rob cleared his throat. "Um, she says so. But I noticed she wasn't lifting anything this morning."

"That means her back is really hurting. She shouldn't have carried Hawk's water bucket last night." Becky looked into Rob's sky-blue eyes. "How are you going to manage crewing for me *and* Tara by yourself?" She'd been counting on her mother to look after Tara.

"Don't worry, you and Windy are my first responsibility," Rob promised.

"I didn't mean that!" Becky said quickly, but she did mean it, she realized. She wanted Rob all to herself on this race. She was depending on him to get Windy safely through the vet checks, and she wanted all his focus on them.

"It's okay." Rob gave her arm a squeeze. "Laurie also said to remind you not to let Windy get caught up with the front runners. You can hold her back and start a little later, according to the race rules."

"That means Mom doesn't think we have a chance to win," Becky sighed. "She's acting like a mother, not a competitor. She doesn't want me getting hurt in the crush."

"I think it's more likely she doesn't want to risk Windy getting hurt," said Rob. "She's been talking to a few other crews. There are some hotshot riders in this race. They'll set a fast pace and probably use fancy strategies to stay ahead. You'll have to be sharp."

Becky could see the other riders bunching around the race officials at the brow of the hill, waiting for the signal to start. "I'll be careful," she promised Rob. "But I'd better get going."

He gave her a boost back into the saddle. "The first part of the race goes down that hill, through dense forest and some swampy stuff." He pointed at the map. "There are places for Windy to drink here, and here." He stabbed the ride map with his finger.

"Let's go!" Tara rode past them on Hawk, her hair streaming back from under her borrowed helmet. Hawk looked ready to fly.

"Go ahead!" Becky yelled to her. "I'm going to wait till after the crush."

"Chicken!" Tara threw the challenge over her shoulder.

Rob stared after her. "She's going to tire Hawk out before they even start."

"I know. She's a bit weird, don't you think?" Becky had no time to wait for Rob's answer. The race master's arm was raised, ready to give the signal to start.

"I'd better go and at least get Windy in position."

"Right." Rob patted her leg. "Your mom had one last instruction. She told me to tell you 'Soft eyes. Remember, soft eyes.'"

"Got it." Becky grinned down at him. "See you at the first vet check."

As she rode toward the start, Becky put her mom's advice into action. Instead of focusing like a laser beam on the race master's signal, she let her eyes go soft and take in the whole scene: the sun kissing the soaring peaks of the Rockies, the green meadow full of horse trailers, the horses poised to run. The beauty of it all steadied her. She took deep breaths and leaned forward to pat Windy's neck. "You keep your eyes soft, too."

"You may start the race!" The signal was given and the horses bunched on the hill took off as if burst from a water balloon. They spurted down the slope in a tight formation, running hard. Some bucked and plunged as their riders tried to hold them back.

Becky fought Windy's urge to race with the others. "Steady, girl!" She turned the mare's head as they had done in practice, sitting deep in the saddle, squeezing the reins, holding her back.

She glimpsed the red ribbon on Hawk's tail in the center of the mass of flying legs hurtling down the hill. Tara was going flat out.

Windy fought loose from Becky's restraint. All her instincts were telling her to run with the other horses—

keep up in case they were fleeing from some terrible danger. Run, run as fast as she could.

Hooves thundered around them. The old terror surged up and filled Becky's throat. Fear of horses—a horse running wild. She had been bucked off a horse when she was four and had never completely gotten over it. She could fall. She could be trampled by those flying hooves!

Desperately, she tried to turn Windy's head, but it was like trying to turn a freight train.

CHAPTER 5

MUDDY WATER

Becky leaned forward and clutched Windy's mane. *Just hold on and stay centered.* She could hear her mother's voice in her mind. *Better to let Windy run than fight her.*

They rocketed down the hill in a blur of flying feet.

At last, the bunched horses stretched out into a line as the leaders galloped ahead. Becky felt the breath return to her body, and she sucked in large lungfuls. Less dangerous now, but still too fast, much too fast for horses who had to run fifty miles up a mountain!

Ahead of her, Becky glimpsed a flash of red in a streaming tail.

Hawk. That's who Windy was chasing.

"Keep away from his back hooves!" she heard Tara shout as Windy drew even with her.

"Windy wants to run with Hawk," Becky yelled back. "And nobody can haul on a horse's reins for six hours! Try to slow Hawk down. I don't want Windy to go this fast. She'll just burn out, or get injured."

Tara gave her a look of total scorn, but she pulled back on Hawk's reins. Most of the other horses passed them, but he seemed happy to stop galloping now that Windy was beside him.

"Is that slow enough for you?" Tara asked breathlessly. "The others are getting way ahead." The leaders of the pack had already reached the trees at the bottom of the hill.

Becky had settled Windy into a comfortable lope. "Look," she panted at Tara, "Hawk and Windy want to run together. They're herd bound because they were penned near each other last night. If you and Hawk want to stay with us, stay at our speed. If you don't, I'll hold Windy back until you're out of sight."

"No. Rob said if I wanted to win, I should pace Hawk and not let him go flat out at the beginning. He said I should stay with you and Windy." Tara shook her head. "But she's so slow!"

Becky couldn't help feel a stab of betrayal that Rob should be so helpful to Tara. "Then go ahead—" she started to shout, but at that moment two horses loped up behind them on a curve. It was Gwendolyn and Graham Belmont, both on bay Arabs that looked identical except for a white star on Graham's horse, Omar.

Becky took the inside edge of the track to let them

pass. Behind her, she could hear Hawk snort and threaten to kick as they gave him a wide berth.

"Hawk hates being behind," Tara protested. "Did we have to let the Gee-Gees shove us off the trail like that?"

"They weren't shoving," Becky snapped back at her. "I chose the inside, where the footing is better, and made *them* go around *us*. Look after your own horse—that's the rule."

Soon they were in the trees, and the trail was only wide enough to go single file. Hawk settled in behind Windy, but Becky could feel Tara's impatience, like a wave pushing them forward.

"Is it true Rob's just a friend?" Tara asked boldly. "He acts like he's your boyfriend."

Becky shrugged her slender shoulders. "If you say so."

"But, I mean, do you like him, or what? You're acting awfully cool about it."

If she only knew. Becky felt anything but cool! "We've been hanging out for a while," she muttered. "He worked at our ranch all summer, helping my dad."

"I guess he helps you, too," Tara laughed. "He seems to know a lot about endurance riding."

"Yup," Becky agreed.

"So, you're not going to tell me," Tara sighed. "It's *your* mystery, like the Belmonts are mine."

"Do *you* have a boyfriend?" Becky steered the subject away from Rob.

"Hawk is the only guy I have time for right now," Tara said proudly. "My horse is my whole life."

Well, I wish you'd act that way when Rob's around, Becky sighed to herself. She thought about Tara's question—how *do* I feel about Rob?

He was the first guy she'd even had a crush on—she thought she might even love him—why else would she get so crazy jealous when he smiled at Tara?

Becky felt sick at the memory. Ugh! Feeling jealous was like having a dragon rear its ugly head and snort fire inside you. It wrecked everything.

She snapped herself back to the present. Just as her mom had warned, Windy was drooping with her negative thoughts. Her ears were down, her pace slower.

"Come on, girl," she urged. "There's a spot to drink just ahead. Let's go."

The watering hole was a stream that trickled into the swamp they'd just passed.

The footing was muddy, already churned up by the faster horses that had stopped for a drink and gone on.

"We'll ride upstream as far as we can," Becky told Tara.

"Why? It's quicker to let Hawk drink here." Tara had guided her horse to the center of the stream, just off the trail.

"Because the water is fresher up there," Becky explained. She rode Windy up the stream to where the water ran faster.

"Oh, all right," Tara grumbled, steering Hawk to drink below Windy. "But Hawk isn't even thirsty, and those Belmonts are getting too far ahead."

"If the horses don't drink, they'll get dehydrated."

Tara stared impatiently as Becky dismounted, filled a syringe with water and a dose of electrolytes and shot it down Windy's throat.

"Why do you bother using that stuff?" she muttered. "You're just wasting more time."

"Look at the white on his coat." Becky pointed to patches of white crust on Hawk's dark hide.

"From sweat, that's all. He's been running hard."

"Right. Horses sweat when they run. And they lose salt in their sweat. That white crusty stuff is sodium and potassium. Electrolytes replace that." She turned to face Tara. "I know Dr. Harris told you not to use your electrolytes," she said, "but this stuff is safe. I have enough for Hawk."

"No, I don't think so." Tara shook her head.

"Suit yourself." Becky stuck the syringe back in her saddlebag. Windy lowered her muzzle into the clear stream and drew in deep satisfying mouthfuls. Two more horses appeared at the stream. They were both Arabs, one almost pure white, the other flecked with gray. Their riders nodded a greeting as the horses bent to drink.

Hawk lifted his head, gave a challenging whinny and began to paw at the stream.

"Don't let him do that!" Becky leaned over and grabbed Hawk's bridle to pull him away from the water.

"What are you doing?" Tara hissed. "What's wrong with you?"

"Hawk's muddying the water for those horses downstream, that's what's wrong." Becky glared at Tara. "In an endurance race, it's bad stream etiquette to do that."

"Bad *stream* etiquette?" Tara rolled her eyes. "What is this? A ladies' tea party? Hawk and I are here to win. What do we care if the other horses drink muddy water?"

Becky didn't answer. She steered Windy away from the stream, hopped into the saddle and started up the trail. How did you explain to someone like Tara that someday it would be her horse drinking from the middle of the stream, and she'd be grateful to a rider who didn't let her horse turn the water to mucky sludge?

"I don't know why you bother to race if you don't try to win," Tara grumbled behind her.

"Who says I'm not trying to win?" Becky turned in her saddle. "Let me ask you something. How did you get into endurance racing?"

The tall girl shrugged. "It was the best sport for Hawk," she said. "Arabians are bred for long-distance riding. I guess with a mixed breed like Windy you have to be more careful. But Hawk was born to run across deserts all day long."

Becky could feel her cheeks getting hot and red, but she ignored the insult to Windy. "I mean," she said, "you don't seem to know much about the sport. Is somebody in your family or one of your friends into endurance?"

"No!" Tara threw back her head. "My twin brothers

are hockey players, and my dad spends all his time, when he's not working at his construction company, driving them to games. And you've seen my mother—she couldn't be less interested. Riding is *my* thing."

She pulled Hawk ahead, squeezing Windy off the trail. "I've already told you," she called as she passed, "Hawk and I are going places. We're going to see the whole world! I may not know much about this *sport*, as you call it, but I think Rob and your mother are wrong. I'm not going to win any races poking along at the speed of a quarter horse nag. Windy's too slow for us."

With that, Tara gave Hawk a kick and he took off at a gallop.

Becky held an anxious Windy back until they disappeared around a bend. "Forget that dark handsome Hawk," she told Windy sternly. "We're better off on our own."

It crossed her mind that Tara would get to the first vet check before her and have Rob all to herself, but she forced that thought from her mind.

"Check Windy's heart rate," she ordered herself, glancing at the dial on her wrist that registered the readings from the heart monitor under the saddle. It was 120, a good, steady working rate, so she gave Windy a little nudge to pick up speed.

Rob was getting ready to drive to the first vet check, loading the truck with water and gear, when he heard

Becky's paint, Shadow, neigh piteously to him from the picket line.

"Sorry, Shadow, you can't come." Rob put down the bucket of grooming gear and walked over to scratch the mare under her long, silky forelock. "I know you're just itching to run with those other horses."

Shadow swiveled her ears to listen to his words.

"I'm going to miss you when I go back to Horner Creek." Rob stroked her side, with its bright brown patches against an almost pure white background. "I'm going to miss everything about Mustang Mountain Ranch, especially Becky."

Shadow bobbed her head up and down.

Rob laughed. "You know Becky's name, don't you?"

He straightened Shadow's silver mane. Like the manes of most mustangs, it flopped every which way on her neck.

"We'll have to braid that mop before you do any endurance rides next summer," he chuckled, then stopped. "What do I mean *we*? I don't know if I'll be back at Mustang Mountain next year. I might not see Becky again till ..."

He paused, picturing Becky's familiar heart-shaped face and warm smile. It was hard to imagine not seeing her every day. "I wish she'd come and live at Horner Creek this winter," he sighed. "But I guess it would be tough, living with Alison and her mom."

Becky's cousin Alison Chant was so different from Becky that it was hard to believe they were related.

Alison had been brought up spoiled and pampered in the east, while Becky was growing up tough and strong on western ranches. No wonder they didn't get along.

Becky's only flaw, as far as Rob was concerned, was how fast she lost her temper. She was overreacting about Tara. Some of that was his fault. He'd been too friendly. But Tara had those flashing eyes and that way of looking at you...

Enough thinking about Tara! Rob gave Shadow a final pat. "Time I got to the first vet check," he told the little mare. "I'll be back soon."

CHAPTER 6

FIRST VET CHECK

"Hey, Windy-girl." Becky leaned forward to pat Windy's neck. "Finally, we're riding *our* race." She paid close attention to the trail markers, turning right on a red ribbon to a rocky trail that snaked along a ridge. Here, she slowed Windy down and was careful to balance her on the rough footing.

She could feel Windy perk up with her own change in mood. Her ears were pricked forward and she moved with an easy rhythm, as if to say, "Now we're cookin'." The air smelled fresh and sweet as they climbed, and Becky felt her spirits rise.

She should have known it wouldn't last.

Heading down the ridge, she saw a brown horse by the trail and a woman bending over to examine the horse's right forefoot. Becky pulled to a halt. "What's the matter?"

"Oh!" The woman straightened up. She was chubby and short, out of breath, with a very red face. Her helmet slid to one side. "I'm so glad you stopped. Tanzer has thrown a shoe." The brown horse was another aristocratic Arabian with a dish-shaped face and short body. He looked worried.

"I guess this is the end of the Wildflower for us," the woman mourned. "These awful rough rocks—I dare not go ahead with no shoe."

Becky took a deep breath. "I've got an easy boot in my bag." She leaned back to unfasten her saddle bag.

The short woman beamed, then frowned. "Oh, but you might need it, dear. This is just the beginning of the race. I couldn't—"

"It's all right." Becky handed the temporary horseshoe down to the woman.

"Thank you," she said. "But I'm not sure I know how to put this on, and I couldn't ask you to help. That would slow you down even more!"

Becky could hear her mother saying, "Endurance racing is all about helping one another." She slid from Windy's saddle and helped fasten the easy boot over Tanzer's hoof. She didn't mind parting with the easy boot so much as losing the time and breaking the rhythm of her ride.

"Did you see a blond girl go by on a dark gray?" she asked as she climbed back in the saddle.

The woman was struggling to get Tanzer close enough to a rock so she could hoist herself into the saddle. "Oh, yes, she went right by," the woman said. "Lovely horse."

Of course Tara wouldn't stop to help! Becky gritted her teeth, then remembered that her anger and frustration would go straight through to Windy. No negative thoughts, she promised, making herself take deep breaths. Good air in, bad air out.

"Good luck," she told the woman. "See you at the first vet check."

"You're an angel. Tanzer! Stand still!"

Becky rode on. A quick look at her watch told her it was only ten o'clock, but the heat was already intense. The next trail marker was a blue ribbon tied to a spruce tree. That meant a left turn.

She pulled the trail map out of her pack to double-check her position. Her mom had told her how easy it was to lose focus, miss a turn and get lost. Becky was determined not to let that happen.

It should be a narrow track, leading off at an angle. There it was—just ahead. She could see the tracks of many horses in the soft ground.

"C'mon, girl," she urged Windy. "Just a few more turns before the first vet check."

Rob watched Tara ride into the vet check area with a surge of relief that quickly turned to worry. Where was Becky?

Tara threw herself off Hawk's back and began to strip

off his saddle. "He needs water," she announced. "Fast!"

Rob placed a bucket of clean water in front of the tired horse. "Isn't Becky with you?"

"Come on, Rob!" Tara was almost shouting. "We have to get him cooled off. He's boiling!"

Rob seized a scoop he'd made out of a large plastic jug and scooped water out of another bucket. He handed a dripping sponge to Tara. "You do his back and legs, I'll do his neck." They deluged Hawk with water. This was where the Arabian breed excelled. They cooled off faster than other horses.

"His heart rate was over 160 at the end," Tara gasped. "And we have to get him down to 64 beats per minute. More water!" She squeezed the water out of the sponge on Hawk's back, then bent to soak it again.

"Why did you ride him so hard?"

"I didn't know the blasted vet check was coming up so fast." Tara sloshed water under Hawk's belly, aiming for the big blood vessels on the inside of his back legs.

"Becky would have known—why didn't you stay with her?"

"Becky, Becky, Becky! You said I could win if I stayed with her, but she's too slow for me," Tara stormed. "I left her in the dust."

Rob did a quick check of Hawk's pulse and respiration. "Still high." He glanced at Tara. "We'll have to wait."

"But I can't start my thirty-minute hold until his pulse and respiration are down," Tara wailed. "Let's walk him slowly over to the station. It will be down by then."

"I don't think… Tara!" Rob started, but Tara was already leading Hawk away.

"Let's go, boy," she told her horse. "You're all right, aren't you?"

The P&R or Pulse and Respiration station was under a large tamarack tree, already turning an autumn gold.

A vet's assistant timed Hawk's heart rate with a stethoscope and watch while Tara held his restless head, trying to calm him.

The assistant, a young woman named Molly, shook her head. "Sorry, his pulse is still high. You'll have to wait another ten minutes and try again."

Tara's face flushed with anger. "Redo the reading," she insisted in a shocked voice. "It can't be right."

"I'm sorry, there are other horses waiting." Molly shook her head. "I'm sure my results are correct."

"Come on," Rob urged. "Let me try to get his heart rate down while you rest and drink something."

"I CAN'T REST!" Tara's eyes blazed. "This is a vet check."

Rob wished Laurie were there. Tara was making Hawk more nervous with her angry voice and waving arms.

Looking closely at the gray horse as they walked him back to his food and water, Rob could see the signs of fatigue Laurie had warned him to look for. Hawk's eyes were anxious, not bright and eager. His whole body looked tense, and his tail was clamped against his body.

"Was he slowing down on the hills?" Rob asked Tara. "Did he stumble?"

Tara didn't answer. She stood rigidly, helmet in her hand, her sweaty ponytail stuck to her neck, staring across the clearing. "Look," she croaked. "Look at the Belmonts. They've finished their vet check. They've finished their half-hour hold time. They're leaving!" Her voice rose with every sentence. She turned an anguished face to Rob. "They're already back in the race."

Rob nodded. "They came in with the first group."

"But they weren't *with* the first group." Tara's voice was harsh. "They were just a little ahead of me. They must have cheated—taken a shortcut."

Rob stared at her. "You can't be sure of that. Why … ?"

She seized his arm. "I know it sounds crazy, but you have to believe me. Those two would do *anything* to win."

"They look pretty harmless to me." Rob shrugged his broad shoulders. "And they've got a really good crew."

"Of course," Tara said bitterly. "Their crew is their brother, Gregory. He's one of the Gee-Gees."

"The Belmonts know what they're doing," Rob went on. "They didn't ride in here like a pack of hyenas was behind them. They jogged in on foot, leading their horses. That meant their horses weren't carrying extra weight, so naturally their heart rates came down faster."

Despite the heat, Tara was starting to shiver. "I've lost, I've lost," she moaned.

"You haven't lost yet." Rob loosened her grip on his arm. "It's a long race, and anything can happen. But right now, you really have to rest and drink, and eat something. Let me look after Hawk." He paused. "I should give him a dose of electrolytes, if that's okay with you."

"I don't know, whatever you think." Tara seemed to have lost all heart.

"C'mon, you need some water." Rob steered her to the collapsible cart he'd used to haul their gear up the hill from where the crews had parked their trucks. He fished out a bottle of water.

"Drink the whole thing," he ordered, "but slowly. And sit down … here's a chair."

He unfolded a canvas chair from the cart, then went back to work cooling out Hawk and giving him a dose of electrolytes … all the while, keeping one eye on the incoming trail for Becky.

When Becky looked down on the vet check area from the top of the hill, she saw a scene of wild confusion. Crews threw water on horses, drenching themselves in the process. Horses crowded around the P&R station, and near each of the two vets. Equipment was piled under the trees: saddles, buckets, carts, water tanks. Some riders even had awnings set up to shelter their horses and themselves during the half-hour hold time.

Where was Rob?

Becky had been running beside Windy for the last mile. Despite the heat and her weariness, it felt good to move her legs. She could tell Windy enjoyed the rest, too. Not having a rider on her back meant she could stretch out into a slow, comfortable jog. Becky knew, just listening to the mare's breathing, that her pulse rate was slowing down.

Now Windy needed water, inside and out. Where was Rob?

As she ran into the vet check clearing, she saw him bend over Tara's long, lean form, lounging in a chair. Instantly, Becky wanted to turn and run in the opposite direction.

This was the person who was supposed to be waiting anxiously for her to arrive? The guy who'd said *she* was his first responsibility? The jealousy inside her swelled to a big green fire-breathing monster.

Becky's mouth felt hot and dry. Her black riding tights and T-shirt stuck to her body, her running shoes were full of stones, and her whole body shook with weariness.

Somehow she kept going until she was standing right beside Rob and Tara.

"I can see you're busy," she croaked.

"Becky!" Rob straightened up to his full six-foot-three with a beaming face. "Where have you been?"

Becky shook with fury now, not fatigue. "Oh, I've been in this little endurance race. About thirteen miles, up and down hills, on foot the last mile. Don't know why I bothered, really."

Tara sat up slowly. "Hawk had an extra hold," she said tragically. "He almost got pulled from the race."

"I am *so sorry!*" Becky undid Windy's cinch with fumbling fingers. "I can do this myself, Rob. You're busy."

"I was just trying to convince Tara to eat something." Rob reached for Becky's hand.

She jerked it away. "Leave me alone, I can do it." But the saddle, with its sheepskin and extra padding, suddenly felt very heavy, and Becky staggered as its weight fell on her.

"Let me!" Rob took it from her. "You've got to cool Windy down and get her ready for P&R. Don't waste time…"

Don't waste time being a jealous idiot. Becky shook herself savagely. Rob was right. Windy was what mattered here. She reached for a sponge and felt the delicious cool water pour down her arm as she slopped water on Windy's neck. Rob was holding the bucket for the mare to drink. They worked quickly, as a team, the way they had practiced.

"Rob," she gasped, "what's our position?"

"You and Windy are near the front of the middle of the pack," Rob explained. "There are quite a few riders still to come in—they started after that first crazy burst. Some have already burned out from too fast a start, or other reasons."

"Mom would be satisfied if we ended up somewhere in the middle," Becky sighed. "But wouldn't it be great if we were in the top ten?"

"It sure would." Rob counted Windy's heartbeats with his own stethoscope. "I think she's ready for P&R. Let's go."

Molly, the vet assistant, nodded once at the end of her official count. "Sixty beats per minute. Excellent. You can go to the vet check any time during the half-hour hold."

"Let's go now and get it over with," Becky urged.

Rob nodded. "Which vet?"

Becky glanced at the lineups for the vets. Janet's was the longest, but she was the vet Windy had seen before, and she was very friendly and sympathetic. "Mom said to stick with the vet you like," she said quickly. "So let's wait for Janet."

She looked back at Tara, sitting in the chair, her long legs thrust out in front of her. "How long before Tara has to leave?" she asked Rob, not looking at him.

"With that extra hold, she still has almost twenty minutes to go," Rob said. "She's over-riding Hawk, and I can't get either of them to eat anything."

"Well, you'd better get back to Tara and keep trying." Becky couldn't keep the sarcasm out of her voice.

"Becky!" Rob seized her shoulder.

Becky shook him off. "I mean it. Go tend to your blond goddess and her champion horse. Windy and I can do the vet check ourselves."

Rob's fair skin flushed red with anger. "I never thought you'd act like this. Between the two of you, I wish I'd never come."

He turned on his heel and marched away toward Tara.

CHAPTER 7

SURPRISE OFFER

Becky was so furious she was trembling again. How dare Rob lump her in with Tara, that ignoramus! She forced herself to take deep breaths and focus on Janet vetting the horses ahead of them.

When it was their turn, she handed her ride card to the girl who was recording results. She held Windy's warm brown face against her chest and massaged her ears. She could feel her own heart thump as she waited for the vet's announcement.

Janet was all business. "Heart rate sixty. Well within the limit." She moved her stethoscope along Windy's side, then switched to the other. "Gut sounds four."

Good. That meant Windy's entire digestive system was working well. Tired horses had no gut sounds in the four areas the vets measured. Next, Janet pinched a fold of skin just below Windy's shoulder, then let go and counted seconds. If the skin stayed tented too long, it meant the horse was dehydrated.

She did another test on Windy's mouth, pressing her thumb hard against the gum, then watching as the white thumbprint turned pink.

"Capillary refill fine, mucous membranes fine," she sang out. The girl recording filled in the card.

Now, Janet's expert fingers felt carefully along Windy's spine, along her flank, down her legs. "No sore spots, muscle tone good."

She straightened up. "Okay, trot her out and back," she ordered.

Becky held Windy on a loose rein and ran with her to the end of the clearing and back to Janet, who measured her heart rate after a minute's rest. "Excellent." She took the stethoscope out of her ears and smiled at Becky. "Heart rate still sixty."

The business of vetting over, Janet gave Becky a brief smile. "She's doing well, but the toughest part of the trail is still ahead. You're giving her electrolytes?"

Becky nodded.

"Okay, then, have a good ride." She gave Windy an affectionate pat on the rump as Becky led her away.

Now there was nothing to do but wait.

"I can't go back to Rob and Tara," Becky muttered to Windy. "Let's find some real grass for you to munch on."

She turned away from the huddle of horses and

walked up the slope to a spot where Windy could graze on mountain meadow grass.

It wasn't long until she heard the sound of wheels bumping over rough ground.

Becky turned to see Rob with his cart, loaded with a tub of mash for Windy, water and a cooler of food and supplies.

"You're making this awful hard for me, Becky," Rob grunted.

"It's not my fault you were so anxious to crew for the mystery girl."

"What's got into you?" Rob exploded. "I thought this was supposed to be a sport where everybody helps each other."

"Well, some people just take advantage," Becky shot back. "You were supposed to be *my* crew."

Rob hoisted the tub of mash to the ground in front of Windy. "And how has it hurt you and Windy that I'm helping Tara? Just tell me that." His piercing blue eyes met her stormy brown ones. "If I'm willing to take on the extra work, what does it matter to you?"

"Oh, you're willing!" Becky felt jealous rage well up inside her. "You're more than willing when a good-looking girl bats her long lashes at you!"

"I'm not listening to this." Rob set down the cooler with a thud. He left, the empty cart rattling behind him.

Becky slumped to the ground. "What am I doing?" she groaned to Windy. "I'm driving him straight into Tara's long, spidery arms."

Windy made no answer except to take another mouthful of grass and chew thoughtfully.

Becky offered her the mash Rob had mixed. It had apples and carrots mixed with beet fiber in a slurpy mixture. Becky could picture Rob chopping up the carrots, taking care the mix was just right. She opened the cooler. Her favorite power drink, energy bars and peanut butter and banana sandwiches were inside.

Rob had thought of everything.

She was suddenly dying of thirst and hunger. "I'm such an idiot," she groaned aloud. "I've forgotten what Mom told me about drinking enough. Maybe that's why my brain isn't working."

But Becky knew that was only half the reason. As the cool liquid slid down her throat, she watched Rob and Tara tacking up Hawk. The taste of the drink turned as bitter as poison.

She flung herself back on the grass with her hand over her eyes. She could feel the sun blasting down, parching the life out of her.

Then someone threw a cool shadow between Becky and the sun. She sat up, shielding her eyes. In front of her stood a tall, chunky man wearing a baseball cap, black tights and T-shirt. She recognized him as the crew for Graham and Gwendolyn Belmont.

"Good afternoon," he said politely. "I don't want to disturb your rest, but I noticed that you were riding with Tara Kosaric."

Becky jerked to her feet. "I was, but—"

"I wonder if you could tell me how her horse, Hawk, is doing?"

"I don't really know," Becky fumbled. "Why don't you ask her?"

"Eh, well, she isn't exactly a friend of my brother and sister. My name is Gregory Belmont." He gave a little shrug. "We're actually in rather an interesting competition with Tara."

"We're all in it." Becky stared at him. "The Wildflower 50."

"Yes, of course, the endurance race, but this is a little *extra* contest. There's a lot *riding* on this race, if you'll forgive a bad pun. I noticed you're sharing a crew with Ms. Kosaric. So I thought you might have some information—I could certainly make it worth your while."

"Money?" Becky reached for her drink and took a long swallow. "I don't know the details about Hawk," she finally said. "Even if I did, I wouldn't tell you—for any amount of money."

She took hold of Windy's lead rope. "Excuse me," she said, "I have to go and tack up."

"I'll see you at the next vet check," Gregory cried behind her. "If you change your mind ..."

"I won't," Becky whispered to herself. What an awful man! What had Tara got herself mixed up in?

CHAPTER 8

STEEP CLIMB

Becky forced herself to guzzle a whole bottle of water and choke down one of Rob's sandwiches.

She knew her mother would hate to see her let her emotions run away with her like this. If she didn't watch it, that jealous green dragon inside her could ruin the whole race.

"All right, Windy," she told the lively little mare, "you're doing your best, I'll try to do mine." She stroked Windy's warm neck lovingly. "Let's get ready for the next part of this race. We've got another ten miles to the second vet check."

Tara was moving out on Hawk when she arrived back at Rob's base.

Becky watched the willowy blond stuff her time and

ride cards in a pack behind her and signal the timekeeper she was leaving. Tara rode toward the start of the trail without looking back at Rob and Becky.

"I left Windy's feed tub and the cooler in the meadow," Becky said to Rob. "Thanks for the sandwiches... and everything." She wanted to tell Rob she was sorry, but the words stuck in her throat.

"You're welcome," Rob said coldly without looking at her. He gazed after Tara. "I hope she doesn't try to catch the Gee-Gees."

Becky felt a surge of anger that he should care. She gulped it back.

"Did you know there's another Belmont brother, named Gregory, crewing for them?" she asked.

Rob nodded. "Yup—a third Gee-Gee." He turned back to Becky. "Tara sure hates them, and for no good reason that I can see."

"I think there might *be* a reason," Becky told him. "Gregory just tried to bribe me to tell him how Hawk did on the vet check."

"You're kidding." Rob's eyes widened. "Are you sure?"

"Do the words 'I could certainly make it worth your while' mean anything to you?"

"Jumpin' catfish. You're serious." Rob stared at her.

"Tara's involved in some kind of extra competition. Maybe it involves money, or betting. But the ribbons and prizes in endurance aren't worth a lot of money—I don't understand."

"It sounds like she might be in over her head," Rob said with a worried frown. "Will you watch out for her on the trail? I know you don't like her much, but—"

"But you do!" The dragon spat fire before Becky could stop it.

Rob's face clouded. "That's what's eating you, isn't it? You think I *like* Tara. What can I say?" He turned away. "Let's get Windy saddled up. Your hold time is almost over."

Rob looked angry and disgusted. But notice, the dragon inside her whispered, he didn't say he *didn't* like Tara.

Becky headed for the highest, steepest part of the trail with a miserable, hollow feeling in her belly. That look on Rob's face as she rode off—and not one word to wish her luck!

All right, maybe she'd been wrong to accuse him of having the hots for Tara. But if he didn't, why did he get so mad? Angry questions bumped through her brain like the beat of Windy's trot beneath her.

She pulled out her ride map. According to it, she had to go high up one slope of Gladstone Mountain and down the other side to the second vet check. After that, the trail looped back to the third vet check before returning to base camp to end the race.

She came to a fork in the trail marked with a blue ribbon. "Left turn," she said aloud, startled by how loud her voice sounded in the wilderness silence. There were twenty-five riders strung along this trail, but she felt totally alone.

"If Meg and Alison were with us," she told Windy, who pricked back her ears, "this would be fun." Meg was a true friend, and even snobby, pig-headed cousin Alison would be better than this awful emptiness.

"Alison is improving," she carried on her conversation with the mare. "She gave Shadow to me, and she didn't have to do that." Alison was off barrel racing with a new horse right now, probably surrounded by cheering, adoring crowds.

Becky suddenly remembered her mother's warning that loneliness was a huge enemy on the endurance trail. It sapped your strength, and the weakness went straight to your horse.

She fought it back, singing an old song with lots of verses to raise Windy's spirits. "She'll be comin' round the mountain when she comes."

Windy seemed to pick up when Becky came to the chorus, with all the sound effects. "Toot toot! Whoa back! Hi, Babe! Scratch scratch! Chop chop! Yum yum," Becky sang at the top of her lungs.

They reached another fork in the trail. Years ago, the mountain had been logged, and there was a network of old logging roads branching in all directions. After a few turns through the trees, this trail rose almost straight up. Becky slipped from Windy's saddle and struggled up the hill beside her.

Something white along the side of the path caught her eye. Garbage. What kind of sloppy rider left paper in the wilderness? The rule was strict. You packed everything out, even hay and horse manure from the campground.

"Hold on, Windy." Becky bent to scoop up the paper. To her surprise, it was a ride card—Tara's ride card, with Hawk's vet check information.

Becky stood there with it in her hand. The card must have slipped out of Tara's bag. Careless! For a second, just a second, she was tempted to drop it back on the ground. Tara would have a tough time without her card— maybe even be disqualified.

"I can't do that, not even to Miss Willow Twig," Becky sighed. She stuffed the card into her own bag and went on.

The trail leveled out on top of a ridge. Becky climbed back in Windy's saddle. You could get spooked by the silence up here, she thought, feeling the skin on the back of her neck crawl. Was that a grizzly bear behind that tree? Or a cougar on that rocky ledge, ready to spring on Windy? The animals were out there, and this was their world, not hers.

Windy seemed anxious to press ahead. She gave a high whinny, which echoed back from the mountain peaks all around.

Then, an answering neigh came from the other side of the ridge.

Not a cougar or a bear—another horse! Probably Hawk.

"So that's your game," Becky whispered. "You've been

trying to catch up to that speedy Arabian. All right, let's see if we can."

They loped down the ridge, along a stony path through a thicket of trees.

To Becky's total surprise, Hawk was not running ahead of them. He was stopped by the side of the trail, his head down. Tara was beside him, her hand on his withers, her head thrown back in despair.

"It's all right," Becky told Tara. "I found your ride card. It's in my pack."

"My ride card?" Tara stared at her. "What are you talking about? I couldn't care less about my ride card. Hawk is lame."

Now Becky could see that Hawk was favoring his right back leg, refusing to put weight on it. She flung herself to the ground. "What happened?"

"I don't know," Tara groaned. "We were going well, coming down that ridge, when he suddenly started limping like crazy."

Becky looked back at the stony path they'd traversed. "It could just be a stone bruise, or even a stone stuck in his shoe," she told Tara. "Why don't you pick up his foot and look?"

"I tried." Tara's lips were pale. "He won't let me. He tried to kick."

CHAPTER 9

WILL HE KICK?

Becky's mind flooded with the memory of a horse kicking her mother in the back while she was shoeing it. Hawk was a horse that kicked. It could be suicide to pick up his back leg—especially if he was injured and hurting.

"Would you look?" Tara motioned to his hind leg. "I'm scared to try again."

Becky had a strong urge to climb on Windy's back and take off. After all, that's what Tara had done—ridden right past the woman whose horse needed an easy boot. Anyway, why should *she* help Tara? There would be other riders along soon. Or she could ride ahead and send help.

But she knew from years of being a ranch kid that if it was just a little chip of stone caught in Hawk's hoof, he could be all right in minutes. "I … uh …" she started to say.

"Please," Tara said. Her eyes were guarded but pleading.

Becky thought of an excuse. "I'm riding this race for my mother," she explained. "If I stop to help you, we'll lose time." But as soon as the words were out of her mouth, Becky knew what her mom would want her to do in this situation.

"Oh, all right," she gulped. "You hold Hawk's head. And I mean *hold* it! Talk to him—tell him everything's going to be all right. I'll give it one shot. If he tries to kick, that's it."

"Thank you!" Tara went to Hawk's head and held it tight against her body. "You're going to be a good boy now," she told him, and then said some words in another language.

"What are you saying?" Becky asked.

"That was Russian for 'If you try anything funny, you'll never see another pail of oats in your life.'"

"Let's hope it works." Becky stood beside Hawk, facing his tail. Taking a deep, deep breath, she worked her way down his side, her hand stroking his dark gray back, then his flank. She paused before letting her hand smooth his rump.

"Okay, I'm going to pick up your sore leg," she told Hawk. "Don't be afraid. I'm not going to hurt you." Leaning close to Hawk's body, she slid her hand down the back of his leg.

He jerked away.

"Hold him!" Becky ordered Tara. "Keep talking to him."

Using her hands the way her mom had taught her, Becky gently lifted Hawk's hoof off the ground and bent to look. Nothing she could see. Her heart sank. Maybe that flinch away from her meant his leg was really injured. She felt gingerly around the bottom of his foot, holding her breath.

Any second, she expected Hawk to explode into frenzied kicking. She could feel him starting to quiver through the length of his body.

There it was! Her fingers felt the point of a sharp stone. She flipped it out. "We got it, boy," she told Hawk. Still leaning into him, Becky gently lowered his foot. She stepped back, breathing hard, the sweat trickling down her forehead.

"It was a stone," she told Tara. "He should be all right now. Walk him forward."

Tara led Hawk down the trail. He took a few cautious steps and then flowed into his graceful, floating trot.

"This is wonderful." The color had returned to Tara's ashen face as she trotted Hawk back to Becky. "You and I should ride together to the next vet check. We can help each other out."

So far, Becky thought bitterly, all the help had been on her side. Tara was what she called a taker, someone who always took more from people than she gave back. But even her company was better than riding alone.

"Sure." She shrugged. "Here's your ride card."

Tara took the card from Becky's outstretched hand and stuffed it loosely in her saddlebag.

"You should be more careful with that," Becky advised. "Someone *else* might not stop, get off their horse and pick it up for you."

Tara blushed. She buckled up her bag and hoisted herself into Hawk's saddle. He shook his head but stood still.

"I *do* appreciate you helping me with Hawk," Tara murmured in a low voice, "even though you didn't want to." She paused. "What makes you dislike me so much?"

"Nothing." Becky couldn't meet those gray-blue eyes. How could she admit she hated Tara just because she was gorgeous and Rob seemed to like her a lot?

She mounted Windy. "Let's move it. We can't be too far from the next vet check."

The old logging road wound among a stand of twenty-year-old pines planted after the original forest was cut down. It was like riding up a dark forest tunnel, wide enough so they could go side by side.

Windy liked Hawk's company. The two seemed to urge each other on, and Becky knew they were making good time on this leg of the race. She checked Windy's heart monitor. One twenty—no problem there.

The white ribbons tied to low-hanging branches reassured her they were on the right track. Ahead, she saw a red ribbon at a fork in the logging road. It fluttered bright scarlet against the green pine boughs.

"We turn here," she sang out to Tara. They swung their horses to the right.

This trail was narrower and steeper.

"I'll go first," Becky panted. "Windy is good on hills, and I'm afraid Hawk might kick."

"I don't think so," Tara protested. "He likes Windy." But she slipped behind Becky and they went on.

"If this gets any steeper, I'm going to tail Windy," Becky called over her shoulder.

"Is that where you grab her tail and she drags you up?" Tara sounded doubtful. "I don't know if I should try that with Hawk."

"Not if you haven't trained him to do it!" Becky wondered just what training Tara *had* given poor Hawk.

The thin figure of a man wearing riding gear slipped out from among the trees at the fork in the road. No one saw him but a curious raven, high in a pine tree.

He cut the red ribbon off the branch and stuffed it in his waist pack. He had to work quickly. More riders were coming up the trail. He didn't want to throw the whole Wildflower 50 on the wrong path. Just Tara Kosaric and Hawk.

"Too bad the kid on the chestnut mare went with her," he muttered to himself. "I would have guessed she had more sense. But maybe she deserved it, for lending Tara that helmet. It would have been so easy if they'd just held Tara back for not having the proper equipment."

He plunged back through the rows of tightly planted trees to where his horse was tethered.

"I hope you enjoyed the rest," he told Omar, "because we have some time to make up."

As he rode off, the raven gave a hoarse cry and flew away, soaring over the treetops.

Half an hour later, Becky was worried.

The logging road was rougher, with deep rain gullies down its center. What kind of ride planner would send horses over such a trail?

Also, more worrying, by now they should have come to a stream where the horses could drink. Hawk and Windy had been working hard. They needed water.

She slid from her saddle.

"What's wrong?" Tara called from behind her.

Becky walked forward a few paces, studying the ground. "Tara," she asked, "have you seen a white ribbon marking the trail lately?"

"No. But I wasn't paying attention. I was following you." Tara leaned forward to pluck some pine twigs from Hawk's braided mane.

"I don't see any hoofprints." Becky studied the trail closely. "Something's wrong."

She hurried to her saddle pack and fished out the ride map. Tracing their route from the last vet check with her finger, she stopped at the spot where a road snaked up to the right.

"Look—" she showed Tara, "this is the road we're on."

"But it's not part of the ride route." Tara's face clouded. "I don't understand."

"I don't, either." Becky's head was buzzing. "I'm *sure* I saw a red ribbon where we turned. Didn't you?"

"Like I said, I wasn't looking." Tara sat upright in her saddle and glared down at Becky. "Are you telling me we took the wrong trail?"

Becky nodded. "I don't know how, but it looks that way."

Tara jumped off Hawk. "We've wasted all this time?" Her eyes were ice cold. "Why have you done this? You must *really* hate me."

Becky's brain reeled. Tara thought she'd taken the wrong trail on purpose?! She stared into Tara's furious face. "I want to win as much as you do—"

"No, you don't!" Tara interrupted her. "I'm going to lose everything. What are we going to do?"

"I—I'm not sure." Becky tried to force herself to think. "We're off trail and the horses need to drink. We're in trouble."

CHAPTER 10

OFF TRAIL

"We have to go back to the right trail!" Tara grabbed for Hawk's reins. "We'll be so far behind!"

"I'm sorry," Becky mumbled, holding her head in her hands. If only her fuzzy brain would clear. "I don't know what happened. I'm sure I saw a red ribbon."

"You must be hallucinating." Tara reached into her saddlebag and brought out a bottle of water. "Here. Drink."

As soon as the water hit her parched throat, the fog in Becky's head began to lift. "It must be the altitude," she gasped. "I'm dying of thirst!"

She glugged down half the bottle and handed it back to Tara. "You drink, too. We're both dehydrated."

Tara took a quick sip. "We must go back," she urged again.

"No, wait." Becky dropped to the ground and spread the ride map out in front of her. The route was traced in red over a copy of a topographical map of the area.

"Look, Tara, if we go back to where we took a wrong turn, we'll still have a long way to go before Hawk and Windy get to water. If they don't drink soon, we're risking any chance they have of finishing the race, let alone winning it."

Tara knelt beside her. "What other choice do we have?" Her question was brittle with urgency.

"I figure we must be about here." Becky's finger jabbed the map. "If we stay on *this* trail, we should intersect a creek here…" Her finger traced a wiggly line a short distance ahead.

"But that puts us even farther behind," Tara groaned. "Farther from the ride route."

Becky bent lower. "Maybe not. Look here." She followed the dotted line of the logging road with her finger. "If we keep going and take the next left fork and then another left, we should meet the ride route *there*."

She jumped to her feet. "We might not even lose that much time."

Tara was still on her knees, staring at the map.

"But what if the creek is dry?"

Becky knew that was a possibility. It was September, a time of low water, and it had been a dry summer. "We'll just have to hope it isn't," she said quickly.

"Or what if we can't find all these other roads? They won't be marked. We could get lost!" Tara turned a pale face to Becky. "That's what I'm most scared of—getting lost out here. People *die* getting lost in the wilderness every year."

This was a new side to Tara. She was usually so sure of herself. Becky picked up the map. "It's a topographical map," she told Tara. "It should be accurate. Anyway, I'm not afraid of getting lost. All we have to do is keep Gladstone Mountain in front of us and make sure the sun doesn't get behind us and we can't go wrong."

Tara gazed at the rows of dark trees. "How can you be sure?"

"I live in the mountains. I'm used to finding my way around them. It's city people—the kind who go on one hike a year—who get lost."

Tara managed a slanted grin. "That's me, the city girl."

Becky knew anyone could get lost, especially on a cloudy day. But she hoped her confidence would reassure Tara. The older girl seemed paralyzed. She crouched on the ground, hugging her knees.

"Look, it's easy," Becky said. "The sun's almost overhead at noon this time of year." She glanced at her watch. "In the afternoon, if we head west, it should be ahead of us and a little to the right."

She folded the map and stuck it back in Windy's saddlebag. "Besides, Windy has a better sense of direction than I do. I'll bet she could find her way back to the base camp on her own."

"All right, let's go on." Tara stood up wearily and took a long look at Hawk. "We have to find water for the horses. Hawk doesn't look too good." She pinched a fold of his skin. "Look, it stays up in a little tent. That's bad, isn't it?"

Becky nodded. "No time to lose. Let's hope that creek isn't dry!"

Rob drove back to the base camp to refill the water containers and grab more supplies for the second vet check.

Other crews were already doing the same thing when he reached the camp. Rob saw Gregory Belmont mixing mash for the two Gee-Gee horses as he drove by the Belmont rig.

"They sure have the best of everything, that bunch," Rob mumbled to himself. "Big fancy horse trailer and a truck big enough to tow an eighteen-wheeler!"

The Belmonts' trailer had large windows in the crew area, and the horses had expensive portable aluminum fencing. No electric-tape fences for those guys!

Rob found Becky's mom stretched on her back in the sunshine beside the Sandersens' trailer.

"Hi there." She sat up carefully. "Just stretching the old back."

"How is it?"

"Better." Laurie smiled. "How are the girls?"

Rob tried to keep his worries off his face. "They're fine," he said, "but Tara had a bit of trouble getting Hawk through the vet check."

"I was afraid she'd ride him too hard!" Laurie frowned. "I sure hope she doesn't wreck that horse."

"Windy was in top condition, though." Rob went over the details of Windy's check.

"That's good. Sounds like you're doin' fine without me."

Laurie stood up and brushed the dry grass off her back. "I had a talk with Tara's mother while you were gone. They have big plans for Hawk."

Rob's ears pricked up. "What did she tell you?"

"Well—" Laurie handed Rob a cold drink from the cooler beside the trailer, "it seems Tara's father is in the construction business in Calgary. Before he came to Canada, one of his jobs was building a pipeline for an oil sheik from the United Arab Emirates."

She took a bottle of water for herself and twisted off the top. "This oil sheik is really into endurance racing. He's been looking for North American Arabians to race against his champions in the desert."

Laurie paused to take a sip. "According to Tara's mother, he wants this race to take place in December. Tara is hoping he'll choose Hawk. Apparently, he'll pay for horse transport and all the travel expenses for Tara and Hawk to go over. On top of that, there are huge prizes for the horse that wins the race."

"Did Tara's mom mention the Belmonts?" Rob asked. "Some kind of bet?"

"No." Laurie stared at him. "Are they part of this Arabian race?"

"Maybe. One of the Belmonts tried to bribe Becky

into spilling information on Hawk." Rob related what Becky had told him about Gregory Belmont.

Laurie bit her lip. "I don't like the sound of that, Rob," she muttered. "I think I'd better come with you to the next vet check. I can drive the truck."

"Good idea." Rob was relieved Laurie felt well enough to help.

"I have another idea." Laurie walked over to scratch Shadow between the ears. "Why don't you ride Shadow to the next vet check? She's bored out of her mind being tied to this picket line. She's practically pawing a hole to China. It would be good for her—a nice run, and not too far."

"Sure," Rob agreed. "Shadow is nice and fresh. It shouldn't take me long to ride up the main road to the second vet check."

He hoisted a spare saddle and bridle out of the trailer and walked over to Shadow, who turned and looked at him as if to say, "This is more like it. When do we leave?"

CHAPTER 11

SHORTCUT

"At last—the creek!" Becky panted. She pointed to a narrow gully across the trail below. Green bushes marked the water course.

"I don't hear any water running," Tara gasped.

They had been leading the horses uphill. Now they started to run down the slope. Their hooves made almost no sound on the soft pine needles, but their breath came in dry, harsh snorts.

Becky knew that if they hadn't taken the wrong trail, Windy and Hawk would have had water almost an hour ago. This was her fault!

She tried not to think of all the terrible things that could happen to a dehydrated horse, from colic to total collapse. There *had* to be water in that creek.

Ahead of her, she heard Tara's howl of despair. "It's dry!"

The creek bed looked empty. Just round, dry stones in a narrow ditch.

Tara was almost crying. She stood beside Hawk's drooping head, his reins in her hand. "No water, Hawk," she said in a heartbroken voice. "What are we going to do?"

Becky studied the sides of the creek bed. Lush green plants grew in a tangle above the rocks.

"Wait a minute." She handed Windy's reins to Tara.

"What are you doing?" Tara stared.

Becky was lifting stones the size of footballs, grabbing them with both hands and tossing them aside as if they were gravel.

"I think… there's water… under here," she grunted. "Look!" She straightened up to show Tara. "The sand is damp."

"So? The horses can't drink damp sand." Tara still sounded desperate.

"No, but this could mean there's water below the surface." Becky knelt to dig at the sand with both hands. "I wish I had a shovel!"

Frantically, she scraped a shallow hole between the rocks, then sat back on her heels, waiting.

Slowly, slowly, a bit of muddy water appeared in the hole. "Water." Becky grinned up at Tara. "Help me make this hole deeper."

Tara swiftly tied the horses to nearby trees and slid down the creek bank to help Becky.

Becky noticed that Tara was sacrificing her fiberglass fingernails clawing at the sand. Her own hands were scraped raw from the rocks.

It was worth it. In a few minutes, they had a hole wide enough for the horses to drink from, with a puddle of muddy water forming in the bottom.

"It's so dirty!" Tara groaned. "Hawk won't drink that."

"Fussy guy, huh?" Becky sighed. "Windy must have mustang blood in her, because she'll drink whatever water she finds, like a wild horse. Anyway," she soothed Tara, "just wait. The water will clear. It's coming up through clean sand."

"Maybe, but ..." Tara glanced at her watch.

"I know. The time." Becky looked at her stricken face. "We'll have to be satisfied with completing the Wildflower 50 and getting Hawk and Windy out of here healthy."

"I can't be satisfied with that!" Tara cried. "It's okay for you—you're just racing to help your mother. But I—" She stopped.

"If my mother were here, she would tell you exactly the same thing," Becky shot back. "She'd say you don't do endurance racing to hurt your horse. You have to do it for the adventure, and just to learn something new every time you go out."

"That's not my idea of a race." Tara clattered up the loose rocks to untie Hawk. "There must be something we can do to go faster."

"We can give the horses electrolytes while we wait for

the hole to fill," Becky suggested. "That'll make them want to drink more."

Tara nodded miserably. They dosed Hawk and Windy, who seemed glad to get any liquid, even from a syringe shoved down their throats.

A few minutes later, the small pool of water was as clear as Becky had predicted. She let Tara and Hawk go first and watched in satisfaction as he sucked up his fill. There was still lots for Windy.

Once the horses were watered, the girls rode off. Becky held the map in front of her on the saddle. They couldn't afford any more wrong turns. She took a fix on Gladstone Mountain, whose peak poked above the trees. The first left fork should be coming up soon.

It was almost invisible. Tree branches overlapped, hiding the old road. Becky brushed them aside, revealing two faint tracks heading south.

"This will be tough going," she told Tara. "Watch out for dead lower branches. They're sharp if they break."

"We'll never get through there." Tara shook her head. "Maybe we should just go back." She turned and looked down the trail they'd climbed.

"Maybe we'll have to—but this is worth a try."

They fought past a screen of tangled brush into the depths of an old planting, where the trees grew so close together almost no light reached them. Only the old logging road gave them enough space to ride single file. Even then, they had to ride slowly, stopping to break off dead branches in their way.

After half an hour of hard going, they broke into a patch of younger pines, only as high as their horses' heads, with lots of space in between.

"It's a new planting," Becky cheered in relief. "This will be easier."

The horses, pleased to be in the open again, picked up a trot.

"Where do we go from here?" Tara sang out.

Becky searched the bouncing map. "There should be another left turn—won't be too far."

Rob jogged Shadow into the second vet check area and staked out a good spot where he could see riders coming in. He made sure there was enough room for Laurie to park the truck, and for Becky and Tara to work with the horses.

Now there was nothing to do but wait. He stripped Shadow of her saddle and led her up a slope to tether her near good grass. She whickered in delight. The half-hour ride had just warmed her up.

Rob stroked the mustang's well-muscled shoulder. Shadow is almost as well conditioned as Windy, he thought. I'll have to talk to Becky about how she plans to keep up with her conditioning this fall—

But I'm leaving tomorrow, Rob thought with a sudden

pang. I won't have time to talk to Becky about anything. If she's even speaking to me. He swung away from Shadow and strode back to the spot he'd staked out to watch the incoming trail.

The ten front runners arrived. Rob saw how smoothly their expert crews took over cooling the horses, letting them drink and settle down before the pulse and respiration check. With these crews, there was no shouting and rushing around—just calm, quiet efficiency.

As they were led to the vet check, the horses swished their tails. They were used to the routine, comfortable being lined up with other horses, examined, poked, prodded and trotted out. They behaved like royalty. If nothing went wrong in the last half of the race, Rob thought, any one of these horses could win.

A few minutes later, Laurie bumped into the field in the pickup. He waved her to their spot. "Any sign of the girls?" she asked as she stepped out of the cab.

"No, but it's too soon. The front runners are just in—" Rob stopped in amazement, staring at the incoming trail.

Coming toward him at a jog were Becky and Tara—together!

Rob turned to Laurie with a puzzled frown. "How did they do it? They must have passed the Belmonts and lots of other riders who left before them."

"I don't know." Laurie shook her head. "But they look like they've been dragged by an ox!"

Tara was staggering with exhaustion. Both of them were covered with dirt and had scratched faces and torn shirts. They stopped at the timekeeper, bent double, their hands on their knees, gasping for breath.

"I'll get Windy," Laurie told Rob. "You look after Hawk."

As Rob raced toward them, the timekeeper logged the girls in, calling out the time so Rob would know how many minutes until they could leave for the next leg of the race.

CHAPTER 12

TARA'S SECRET

"Rob!" Tara straightened up, one hand on her pounding heart. "I've never been so glad to see anyone in my life."

Becky looked from Tara's rapturous face to Rob striding forward to take Hawk's reins.

He picked Tara to help first, not her! The green dragon shot a spurt of flame that turned the whole scene to gray ash.

"Your mom came, too," Tara gasped happily. "And they brought your cute little mustang."

Cute little mustang? Only Laurie, hurrying toward her, kept Becky from screaming at Tara.

"What happened?" Laurie grabbed Windy's reins. "You two look like you crawled up the mountain."

"We almost did," Tara blurted. "Becky took a wrong

turn. We got so lost, but then we found a shortcut." Her face clouded over. "Are we very late?"

"Late?" Rob shook his head. "You're way ahead of—"

"The Belmonts?" Tara's face lit up like a halogen lamp. "Am I ahead of the Gee-Gees?" She gripped Rob's arm. "Tell me!"

Rob nodded, still with the puzzled frown on his face. "It looks like it."

Becky stared from one to the other. On top of blaming her for getting lost, on top of grabbing Rob like he was her personal hero, after all that had happened, Tara still only cared about beating the *Belmonts*? Hadn't the brain-dead girl learned anything?

"Come on," Laurie urged. "Let's get these horses cooled out."

Tara was still holding Rob's arm. "Will you take care of Hawk?" she begged. "I want to go and gloat in front of the Gee-Gees."

"No, stay with us, Tara," Laurie told her firmly. "We *all* need to cool the horses. And you two need to drink and clean up." She turned to Becky with a worried frown. "Once we've done that, you'd better tell me about this shortcut you took."

As they walked the horses to the truck, Rob leaned close to Becky to ask, "How did you end up riding with Tara?"

"Hawk picked up a stone, and Tara was too scared to get it out herself. I had to stop to help her." Becky kept her eyes straight ahead.

"That was ... so nice of you. I'll bet you were more than a bit scared, too."

He had that right! Of course, Rob would know how frightened she was of horses that kicked. He knew so much about her. Becky took a deep breath. "Look, Rob, I'm trying. I don't want to fight with you. It's just ..." She turned to face him.

"It's okay ... the stress of the race ..." Rob blushed to the roots of his pale blond hair. "Do you want to—talk about it?"

"Not now." Becky knew that Rob knew perfectly well it was more than race stress that was bothering her. But she couldn't talk about Tara without flaring up all over again.

Anyway, she had something else to worry about. That look on her mom's face when she heard about the short-cut, and getting lost. What did it mean?

"According to the rules," Laurie said as she sponged Windy's flank, "you should have retraced your steps back to the ride route. I'm afraid you'll both be disqualified."

Becky could see disappointment written all over her mother's face. Disqualified! She felt like she'd been punched in the stomach. How could she have forgotten the rule—no riding off trail?

"I think you did the right thing, though." Laurie plunged her sponge into the water tank. "Hawk and Windy needed water and you went to the nearest creek."

"But once the horses drank, we should have ridden back to the fork where we went wrong," Becky groaned. She knew her mom was trying to make her feel better, but it wasn't working.

"It was your first race," Laurie sighed. "It's easy to get confused."

"I was so sure I saw a red ribbon." Becky threw down her sponge. "I can still see it in my mind."

"I told you we should go back to the trail." Tara sloshed water over Hawk's back with the plastic scoop. "But it doesn't matter. We're here, and I'm ahead of the Gee-Gees."

"What do you mean, it doesn't matter?" Becky glared at her.

Tara raised one eyebrow mysteriously. "I told you—there's more at stake for me in this race than a prize ribbon."

"About that..." Laurie frowned. "Your mother and I had a long talk. I'm afraid your big secret is out of the bag."

"She told you?" Tara's smooth forehead creased in an angry frown.

"What?" Becky looked from one to the other.

"You're usin' the Wildflower 50 for another purpose. And, if I guess right, the Belmonts are involved, too. Is that right, Tara?" Laurie's brown eyes were challenging. "Whoever wins gets a trip to the Middle East with their horse?"

Tara nodded. "The sheik's agent came to the stud farm that bred Hawk and the Gee-Gees' Arabians, Omar and Ali Baba. He said he would pick the best horse from that bloodline."

"That's the great mystery?" Becky gaped at her. "That's why Gregory Belmont was so interested in Hawk?"

Tara gazed off into the distance. "It will be wonderful," she sighed. "The sheik's family imports pure vicuña cloth from South America to make blankets for their horses. They cost thousands of dollars."

"So?" Becky's hands were on her hips.

"So—" Tara gave a determined shrug. "I want to see all of that. I want to feel the softest horse blankets in the world. I want to fly with Hawk to the real Arabia, where he comes from, and race with him against the best." She shrugged again. "Then I can prove to my father that not only boys do big things like becoming famous hockey players. Girls can do great things, too."

Graham and Gwendolyn Belmont gasped with the effort of running the last part of the trail beside their Arabians.

They stopped, stunned, at the sight of Tara and Hawk, already walking to the Pulse and Respiration station.

"Look at her!" Gwendolyn glared at Tara from across the field. "She's ahead of us!"

"I just can't understand it." Graham shook his head. His sparse gray hair was plastered to his scalp with sweat. "I tied a red ribbon... I saw her take the wrong trail. How did she get here first?"

"I don't know, but she did," Gwendolyn said as they panted up to their brother, waiting with water buckets and scoops. "And her horse, Hawk! He looks in better condition than he was at the last vet check. What's her secret?"

Gregory had been waiting for this moment. "I think I know," he announced, grinning widely. "Look what I've got." He held up a plastic bag full of white powder. "This is the electrolyte mixture she uses."

"Where did you get that?" Gwendolyn demanded.

"From their trailer." Gregory chuckled. "I thought it might be some kind of miracle stuff, and it must be, judging by how fast Hawk got here."

"Are you sure no one saw you take that?" Gwendolyn reached for the bag.

"No one saw me," Gregory assured them. "The girl's mother was talking to the Sandersen woman over at their rig. She left the back of the trailer open."

"If this is what makes Hawk go so fast, we'll give it to Omar and Ali Baba," Graham said. "We'll give them double doses before we leave this vet check, then some every time they stop for water." He glared over at Tara. "We've got to beat her on this next leg of the race."

CHAPTER 13

SECOND VET CHECK

Janet Harris, the vet, smiled approvingly at Hawk. "He's doing better. Heart rate 52. Good gut sounds. A few scratches and nicks from the trail, but no soreness."

"I've been giving him Becky's electrolytes." Tara's full lips curved in a smile. "I guess the stuff really works."

Janet nodded. "If you use the right kind and use it correctly, it makes a big difference." She stroked Hawk's shiny flank. "Now don't get excited and push too hard on the next stretch. Remember, you have to see me at the third vet check, and then again after the race. Hawk has to pass that final check, too, or he gets disqualified."

"I know." Tara was glowing. "I'm not worried, now."

Becky was next in line. "Tara hasn't said a word

about taking the wrong trail," she murmured to Rob. "What should I do? Should I say something?"

"It's not the vet's job to disqualify you," Rob advised. "Go ahead with the check."

Tara was trotting out Hawk. They made a picture, the girl with the long legs and the flowing ponytail, the horse with his fluid stride and long gray tail.

"A girl and her desert hawk," Becky breathed. She could feel Rob's attention focused on Tara. "No sign of lameness from that stone in his hoof."

"Nothing wrong with Hawk now," Rob agreed.

Tara finished the trot, bringing Hawk back to Janet. His pulse, a minute later, was within the limit.

"Well done." Janet made her final notes on Tara's ride card and handed it to her. "You're clear to go—after your hold. Remember what I said. Pace him!"

But Tara was already triumphantly leading Hawk away.

Becky thought Rob might follow her, but he stayed beside her while Janet checked Windy.

She could feel the grip on her heart loosen as she held Windy's chestnut head and massaged her ears. Windy gave a deep sigh, which was good for her blood pressure and meant she was feeling good in Janet's gentle hands.

Janet listened and counted and felt Windy all over. Then she glanced up at Becky. "Windy's doing well," she said. "Showing the strain of a long run, but she's got a lot left. But how about you? You don't look so good."

"That isn't your job," Becky wanted to say. "I'm not a

horse." But Janet was still looking at her with a veterinarian's piercing gaze.

"I'm okay," she lied. "We got scruffed up in some rough brush—that's all."

"Got off trail?" Janet nodded sympathetically. "It happens every year. Too many old logging roads out there."

She turned back to Windy and fired off her readings to the recording assistant.

"All right," she told Becky, "trot her out for me."

Becky headed down the field, trying to keep from swaying with the storm of her feelings. I've failed, she thought. I got off trail and didn't retrace my steps. Soon everyone will know.

The vetting over, Becky and Rob walked the horses away from the crowded vet check to graze during their hold time. Hawk had kicked out jealously at Shadow—wanting to have Windy all to himself. Finally, they moved him farther up the field.

"I guess he still needs that red ribbon in his tail." Rob shook his head.

"Guess so…" Becky paused, thinking once again of the red ribbon fluttering from the pine branch.

Fluttering—like a real red ribbon, not hanging stiffly, like the usual plastic race ribbons.

"Rob," she said, "there was something funny about that ribbon."

"Hawk's?" Rob looked confused.

"No, not Hawk's. The ribbon where I took the wrong turn. It didn't look right."

"Forget about it," Rob said gently. "Let it go."

"You don't believe me!" Becky gripped his hand. "Nobody believes I saw that ribbon, but it was there. I swear it!"

She gazed at Windy, grazing peacefully. "I can't stand it that I blew the whole race," she groaned. "Mom pretends it's all right, but I know how she really feels. I've let her down. What am I going to do?"

Before hitting the trail for the next part of the Wildflower 50, Laurie and Rob went over the ride map carefully with Tara and Becky.

"A maze of ATV trails crisscross the next section," Laurie warned. "You'll have to watch out for rogue ATV riders. They don't always stick to the trails."

"Shadow and I met a couple, coming up the road," Rob agreed. "Those four-wheelers are so loud they make a mountain road sound like a freeway."

"Then we'll hear them coming." Becky nodded.

Once the ride map was folded and stowed away in her pack, she went to change her sweaty socks and torn T-shirt in the portable outhouse provided for the riders.

Tara was prowling around the pickup when she got back. "You changed your clothes in the middle of the race?!" she cried when she saw Becky. "It's bad luck. In championship series, my brothers never change their hockey uniforms. They don't even let my mother wash their socks."

"You should eat something." Becky handed Tara a sandwich from the cooler. "Or is that bad luck, too?"

"I can't eat." Tara waved it away. "I'm too nervous."

"Well, just to make you more nervous," Becky warned her, "here comes your *enemy*." She couldn't keep the sarcasm out of her voice.

Graham Belmont was striding toward them. He slapped his riding gloves against his thigh.

"Having a good race?" he sneered. "Funny, I didn't see the two of you pass us, yet you got here first." He slapped his gloves again and gave Tara a frosty smile. "I've talked to several other riders and they didn't see you, either."

"I'm not talking about the race with you." Tara drew herself up, long neck extended in a queenly pose.

"Please go away," Becky said. "We're trying to rest."

"As you wish." Graham turned. "I suppose it will all come out at the awards ceremony tonight anyway." He strolled off toward the other Gee-Gees and their horses.

"They know about our shortcut," Becky said. "We're sure to be disqualified."

"I've told you already, I don't care about the silly race rules. If I beat the Belmonts, I win. It doesn't matter how I do it."

Becky looked at her watch. "Our hold time is almost

up," she said. "We should be saddling Hawk and Windy—" she paused, "and you should look for someone else to ride with. Someone who can help you pace Hawk, so you don't ride him too hard and—"

"What about you?" Tara interrupted. She swung around to stare at Becky.

Becky straightened her own spine. She'd thought it over, and no matter what Tara or anyone said, her mind was made up. "I'm going back to the fork where I saw the red ribbon," she announced. "I'll pick up the trail where we left it and ride the race the right way."

"Are you *insane?*" Tara's thin eyebrows shot up. "Why would you do that?"

"Because I want to complete the race properly. We took a shortcut. My mistake. But it means our ride is incomplete. You say it doesn't matter to you if you're disqualified? Fine. Then you'd better go ahead. It matters to me. I'm riding this race for Mom, and I can't let her down." Becky brushed back her tumble of curls. "Besides, I want to see for myself if there's a red ribbon where I turned. I'll bet it's still there."

She picked up her saddle and started off to get Windy. "Don't forget to give Hawk his electrolytes," she shot over her shoulder. "I've given you plenty to last the race. And you should take better care of yourself, too. Don't forget to drink."

CHAPTER 14

LOST POWDER

"I have a great idea, Mom." Becky hoisted Windy's padded saddle into place. "If I go back over the shortcut to pick up the real trail, I'll save time. That would be legal, wouldn't it?"

"Take the shortcut? I suppose so." Laurie helped her tie on her saddle bag. "But you said the shortcut was rough. Are you sure you want to go over it again?"

"There's just a few bad spots." Becky shrugged. "I promise to be careful. Besides, Windy can handle it."

Rob strode over to listen as Tara rode out. "What's up? Tara says there's some crazy idea about you going back to complete the race the right way." He looked from Laurie's worried face to Becky's stubborn one.

"It's not crazy," Becky insisted.

Laurie bit her upper lip. "She wants to ride back to the fork through the pine plantation, but I don't like the idea of her ridin' that shortcut alone. If anything happened, there'd be no other riders to help. You could get lost—" She turned back to Becky. "What if you don't recognize the ride route when you get there?"

Becky frowned. "I'll see the red ribbon on the tree." She glared at her mother. "You think I'll get lost because there *is* no red ribbon on that tree. You think I made it up."

"Becky ... no one's accusing you of any such thing."

"Why don't I ride over the shortcut with you, on Shadow?" Rob broke in. "That wouldn't break any rules, would it? As long as I don't come back on the actual ride route with Becky?"

Laurie looked from one to the other and broke into a smile. "You're right," she said. "That's a good idea."

"Wait here." Rob was already running. "I'll get Shadow saddled."

"He really does care for you, you know." Laurie watched him sprint across the field. "Why are you givin' him such a hard time?"

"If Rob Kelly cares about me, why doesn't he just *say* so?"

"Guys don't always know how to say that kind of stuff." Laurie smiled. "Your father never actually proposed to me. He just always assumed we were getting married. It drove me crazy! The kind of man who falls all over himself with pretty talk isn't the one you want— trust me."

"Maybe you're right. But why does Rob get that stunned look on his face every time Tara comes near?" Becky demanded. "Why is he always rushing to help her?"

"Well, girls like Tara, who look like supermodels—"

"Don't rub it in!" Becky burst out.

"Let me finish," Laurie said sternly. "Girls like Tara affect everybody that way—not only men. But it's just surface. Rob's not dumb enough to fall for good looks and charm unless—" she paused, "unless you push him over the edge by acting meaner than a buckin' horse with a burr under its saddle."

"But—" Becky started.

"But nothing! You've been about as friendly as a rattlesnake since Tara showed up," Laurie scolded. "I wouldn't blame Rob for turning to someone who seems to appreciate all he's doin' for her."

"But I get so mad!" Becky rested her forehead on Windy's saddle.

"It's normal for riders to be grouchy to their crew at endurance races," Laurie went on. "I've seen couples break up over it. But you're worse than grouchy, you're downright mean."

"Enough." Becky raised her hand. She turned a flushed face to her mother. "I get it. I'll try to be nicer."

"Glad to hear it." Laurie reached out and smoothed Becky's tumbled hair. "Whatever happens, I'm proud of you for wanting to complete the ride according to the rules. You've got hold of what endurance racing is all about."

"Not like Tara," Becky began to say.

Laurie's eyes flashed.

"Oh … there I go again." Becky stamped her foot, and Windy gave a little snort and pawed the ground. "I'm sorry, girl." Becky stroked the mare's neck. "No more anger, no more jealous thoughts, I promise."

Once Rob had Shadow ready to go, Becky spread out the map again to show him the route they would take together.

"The first part is pretty easy." She ran her finger up the dotted line of the road. "But here, the trees grow so close together you can hardly see the road. That's where the trouble starts. There's a waterhole here to water the horses." She showed him. "And then this old logging road winds down to the fork. It's steep and really rocky."

"When we get to the ride route, I'll come back here and wait for you," Rob promised. "Then I can help you get Windy ready for the next leg."

"But I'll be so late getting to the third vet check," Becky mourned. "Everybody will have left by the time I get there!"

Laurie looked concerned. "Don't you worry about time," she warned. "Your biggest problem will be isolation, once Rob is gone. Riding alone isn't fun."

"I already know that." Becky nodded in agreement. "Even Tara was better than nobody."

She caught the look in her mother's eye.

"I mean, it was better, riding with Tara," she sighed.

If Rob caught the correction, he didn't let on. "Let's get going," he said. "I've got extra water for you and enough food and electrolytes for Windy for the whole trip. I figure it will be almost eight extra miles."

Becky gulped. That meant she'd ride nearly sixty miles before this day was over. Ninety-six kilometres. Ouch. And poor Windy!

"Are you sure you want to do this?" Laurie asked. "You don't have to."

"Can Windy make it?"

"I think so. If you take it easy. Real easy."

"Then so can I." Becky nodded.

She put her running shoe in the caged stirrup and hoisted herself into the saddle. Windy tossed her head, eager to set out on another leg of the journey. Becky blessed the sturdy little mare, who would give her all if she were asked.

And Shadow, who was still fresh, was almost dancing in her readiness to take to the trail. "You go ahead," Rob told her. "Set the pace."

"Goodbye, Mom," Becky shouted over her shoulder. "Don't worry, Windy will look after me."

"Wish it was me in that saddle," Laurie called back. "Good luck."

In almost no time, the second vet check area had vanished behind them. They were climbing into a forested area that stretched as far as the eye could see in all directions.

The lonely peak of Gladstone Mountain was at their backs.

They loped through the plantation of young trees. Becky kept her eye on the trail—it was easy to miss. Everything looked the same out here. The main thing was not to get lost!

Tara was shocked. Half an hour from the second vet check, she heard horses behind her, riding hard.

"Coming by," she heard.

Remembering Becky's advice, she pulled Hawk to one side of the trail, where the best footing was.

To her total surprise, it was the Belmonts who were overtaking her. Where had they come from?

Gwendolyn on Ali Baba flashed by, then Graham on Omar. The horses' glossy bay coats were shiny with sweat.

Graham turned to grin at her as he passed. The skin on his face was pulled tight by the effort and speed of his ride, and the grin turned into a grimace that made Tara shudder.

"They are *evil*," she hissed to Hawk. "How did they catch up to us? They started so much later."

It was time, she decided, to ignore the veterinarian's advice to pace Hawk. "We've got to catch them," she murmured in his ear, leaning forward to give him the signal to go, go, go!

Laurie drove the truck back to the base camp for more supplies. As she pulled in, she saw Tara's mother, Eva, in her long skirt, waving from the doorway of her trailer.

Laurie sighed as she pulled the truck up to their own trailer. She didn't feel like talking to Eva right now. She was too worried about Becky and Windy retracing all those steps.

But the poor woman was having a long, lonely day, Laurie thought, and she must be worried, too.

"Hi there," Laurie called as she stepped out of the truck.

"Oh, Mrs. Sandersen, I'm so glad to see you," Eva gushed. "How are the children?"

Laurie grinned to herself. Becky would hate being called a child. "They're fine."

"Come in. You must be so tired, and your back must be so sore."

"I'm pretty dusty." The inside of the Kosaric trailer looked like a showplace, Laurie knew. Not a speck of dust or hay or straw to be seen.

"No, never mind, come in. I fix you a cold drink." Eva held open the door, beckoning.

"I'd like to, but I have to load the truck for the third vet check," Laurie apologized.

"Please," Eva begged. "I want to know how my Tara is doing."

"Just for a few minutes, then." Laurie smiled and stepped into the large trailer. "Tara is fine. Hawk's running well."

"The children will come back here, no?"

Eva showed Laurie to the most comfortable chair, an armchair tufted in red.

Laurie nodded. "Yes. The course is a loop."

"About what time, do you think?"

"Between two thirty and three thirty," Laurie told her, perching on the edge of the chair. "If all goes well."

"If? What could go wrong?" Eva's eyes were bright with concern.

"Anything can go wrong in an endurance race," Laurie sighed, then realized she wasn't making Eva feel any better. "But I'm sure the girls will be all right."

"I'm so glad my Tara is riding with your Becky."

Laurie decided she wouldn't tell Eva that Tara was now riding alone. Why worry the poor woman more? It would be safer to talk about Tara's horse.

"Tell me how you found Hawk," she said politely.

Eva beamed. She gushed information about Hawk: how they found the breeder, how they selected him, how he was trained. "Would you like to see his ribbons?" she asked. "We brought them all with us."

She led the way to the back of the trailer, where everything was beautifully neat and organized, including a row of first-place ribbons Tara and Hawk had won in the costume classes at registered Arabian shows.

"Amazing," Laurie breathed.

"But something is wrong," Eva exclaimed. "Something is missing!" She scanned the neat shelves anxiously. "I keep everything right at hand for Tara," she muttered, "so she never has to search for what she needs. Something has been moved from here." She pointed to an empty spot on the shelf, looking puzzled.

How could she possibly remember what was on every single shelf? Laurie wondered.

Eva's face suddenly cleared. "I know. It was the white powder—the electrolytes the vet said Hawk should not take. They were in a plastic container—right there!"

"Are you sure? Maybe Tara threw the container out."

"No." Eva shook her head. "They were on that shelf after she left."

"Well, when you find them, throw them away," Laurie said. "They could be very dangerous to an endurance horse."

CHAPTER 15

PANICKED!

Windy kept a steady pace through the young trees. Becky remembered how her mother said you always learned something from your horse in an endurance race. In this race, she was learning patience from Windy. It didn't matter that they had to retrace their steps and let the others get ahead—the mare moved cheerfully at a slow lope, as if they had forever to finish the race.

Somewhere on the ridge above them and to the right were Tara and all the other riders.

She turned in the saddle and grinned at Rob. He was way too tall for Shadow. The little paint mustang was just over fourteen hands high, and Rob's legs hung down below her belly.

Shadow shook her shaggy head as if to say, "Hey!

Shouldn't you be riding me instead of this big guy?"

"Don't laugh at us," Rob called forward. "We're doing the best we can."

"I'm not laughing." Becky grinned. "I'm just glad you're with me." She slowed so that Rob came even with her. "Especially when I've been such a pain in the rear all day. I'm sorry."

Rob nodded. "It's all right. I guess everyone gets tense in a race."

Neither of them mentioned Tara.

"Up ahead is where the trees grow really close together." Becky pointed to the dark line of forest. "We have to be super careful the horses don't get poked in the eye with a dead branch. Some of them are like spears!"

Meanwhile, Eva Kosaric was banging on the Sandersens' trailer door.

"Mrs. Sandersen ..." she puffed as Laurie swung the door open, "I found that powder. The seal is broken and some is missing. Then I remember—that fat man who just drove in ... he was looking in the back of our trailer while you and I were talking earlier this morning. I saw him— but I was thinking he was just admiring Hawk's ribbons."

She paused to catch her breath, then rushed on, "Maybe the fat man took the powder."

Laurie came down the trailer steps slowly. "Which man?"

"That one." Eva pointed to Gregory Belmont, who

113

was easing his bulky body out of the large truck cab.

Laurie gasped. One of the Gee-Gees, as Tara called them. They were mixed up in this crazy contest with her. If they thought her electrolyte mix had given Hawk an edge, they might try it on Omar and Ali Baba.

"What should we do?" Eva twisted her hands together.

"I'm not sure." To accuse someone of stealing was serious, Laurie thought. On the other hand, if they had taken the electrolytes to use on their horses, the results could be disastrous.

"Come with me," she told Eva as she headed for the Belmonts' rig.

Gregory was just about to disappear inside his trailer.

"Mr. Belmont," Laurie cried, "we need to talk to you."

"What do you want?" He almost snarled as he recognized Laurie striding toward him with Eva hurrying behind.

"Someone seems to have opened a container of electrolytes from Mrs. Kosaric's trailer and taken some." Laurie tried to keep her voice polite. "We thought it might be you."

"Well, it wasn't." Gregory started to shut the door.

Laurie reached out and grabbed the handle. "Janet Harris, the vet, says that those electrolytes are only suitable for racehorses on a short track, Mr. Belmont. If you know who took them, please, tell them how dangerous they are."

"Well! They certainly don't seem to be causing any

harm to Tara Kosaric's horse." Gregory wrenched the door free of Laurie's grip and slammed it after him.

"Wait!" Laurie banged on the door.

It stayed shut.

"I've got to do something," Laurie muttered to Eva. "I'm *sure* he took them." She hurried back to her truck.

Eva struggled after her in her high heels. "What are you going to do?"

"The vets will be at the third check, waitin' for riders to come in," Laurie told her. "I'm going to drive up there as fast as I can. If the Gee-Gees dosed their horses with that stuff, we need to act quickly."

"Oh, dear. Should I come?"

"No." Laurie shook her head. "Stay here and wait for Tara." She jumped in her truck. "It's a good thing you keep track of Tara's equipment so carefully," she said.

"It's all I can do for my girl." Eva shrugged sadly. "I'm not so good with horses."

Becky and Rob threaded their way through the thick pines. Suddenly, off to their right, they heard a loud crashing, as if something large was blundering through the trees.

Becky jerked Windy to a halt. "What was that?"

"Sounds like a large animal—" Rob peered through the dense tangle of branches, "coming this way!"

"Something bad is happening." Becky leaned forward

over Windy's neck to calm her. "Wild animals don't make that kind of noise."

At that second, there was a high whinny of pain and fear. Windy answered with a neigh of alarm.

"Hawk!" Rob and Becky cried together.

"No, it can't be Hawk." Becky shook her head. "Tara was ahead of us, and we're a long way from the main trail."

The crashing and snapping of branches grew louder. "Let's go!" Becky shouted. "Whoever it is needs help."

Stretching forward to push back the dead branches with their hands, she and Rob rode in the direction of the sounds. With no path underfoot, the ground was rough and uneven, strewn with stumps and deadfall from an old fire. It was terrible footing for horses. Becky's T-shirt was snatched and torn by the tangle. It was impossible to go fast.

The wild crashing sounds were on their left, then behind them, then on their right.

"The horse must be panicking," Rob shouted as they turned their horses. "He's all over the place—he could be dangerous!"

In the next moment, Becky saw him—a dark bay Arabian coming straight at her. He was bouncing off the tree trunks, his hide pierced by the cruel dead branches.

Becky recognized the star on his forehead. "Omar!"

Omar's eyes were rolling, his ears were back, and the muscles along his side twitched.

"Stay back." Rob reached for the coiled rope on Shadow's saddle. "I'll try to get a rope on him."

Becky knew there was almost no chance Rob could throw a loop around the neck of a horse in all these trees. Her fear of rampaging horses gripped her, freezing her to Windy's saddle.

"Look out!" Rob shouted. Becky heard the zing of a rope past her ear as Omar continued to rush toward her.

The rope slid uselessly over the bay's back. Becky held Windy's reins and braced herself for the attack.

But a few steps away, Omar staggered and then stopped. Becky could feel her heart thumping wildly as he sank to his knees, shuddering. With a groan that sounded almost human, he collapsed on his side.

"Rob! What's wrong with him?" This was much worse than scratches and puncture wounds!

Rob threw himself off Shadow and knelt by Omar's side. "It looks like some kind of seizure." Rob glanced up at her, his face full of alarm.

Becky felt sick. This beautiful animal—so wounded and helpless. "We've got to get help."

She hopped off Windy and handed her reins to Rob. "I'm going to ride Shadow back to the second vet check, then down the road to the third. Someone should be there."

"I'll go." Rob stood up.

"No, Shadow is fresher than Windy, and I'm lighter on her back." Becky struggled to shorten Shadow's stirrups.

"Let me help." Rob did up the stirrup on the other side. As Becky swung herself into Shadow's saddle, he reached up and gently touched her cheek. "I wish I could go with you. Don't take any chances, but hurry."

"I will." There was no time to say anything else. She looked into Rob's worried blue eyes, then urged Shadow forward, bending low to avoid the prickly branches.

Tara was pushing Hawk hard. They had passed several riders, but there was no sign of the Gee-Gees. "They must be flogging their horses," she said aloud. "I should have caught them by now."

A short distance past the next bend, Tara saw something that made her pull Hawk up with a snort. A thin woman stood in the middle of the trail, waving her arms.

"Gwendolyn Belmont!" Tara breathed in surprise. "What's wrong? Where's your brother—and your horses?"

"Ali Baba bolted sideways!" Gwendolyn cried. "One minute I was sitting on his back, the next I was on the ground. I don't know where Graham and Omar are. I've been running, waiting for someone, anyone, to come along. Anyone but you!"

She gaped at Tara. "This must be a judgment on us. I told Graham and Gregory not to do it. I told them!" She suddenly went white. "Go. Tell someone we need help. I've got to find Ali Baba."

"All right," Tara promised. "I'll tell everyone I meet. I'm sure the ride management will send somebody."

She urged Hawk into a gallop. But a part of her felt uneasy. Should she have stayed to help Gwendolyn look for Ali Baba?

Tara shook off this unfamiliar guilty feeling. "No," she told herself, remembering the woman's bitter look. "She'd never accept my help, anyway. I'd just be wasting precious time."

But as Tara rode along, the image of Gwendolyn's stricken face stayed with her. Hawk seemed to know her mind was wandering. The big Arab slowed to a shuffling walk.

His slow, swaying pace made Tara feel fuzzy and confused. The trail turned and twisted and crisscrossed other trails. She stopped watching for white flags. When she came to a branch in the trail, she followed the more traveled track, which led off to the right. It was carved deep in the sandy soil, and if Tara had been concentrating, she would have seen it was made by two sets of tires, not by horses.

CHAPTER 16

JANET'S JOB

Laurie Sandersen's truck bounced over the uneven ground to the third vet check. On the other side of the field, under an awning rigged up beside a small trailer, she could see the vets and their volunteer helpers relaxing in the shade.

They looked up in surprise to see a pickup hurtling toward them.

"Laurie! Where's the fire?" Janet Harris called as the truck jerked to a stop.

Laurie jumped out of the cab and slammed the door. "Tara's mother thinks she saw Gregory Belmont take electrolytes out of her trailer," she said grimly. "I talked to him, and I think he gave them to the Belmonts' horses."

The smile on Janet's cheerful face disappeared. "Are you sure?"

"I'm not positive, but there's a good chance. You said they were dangerous ..."

"Maybe fatal," Janet groaned. "Ali Baba and Omar were so stressed at the last vet check I thought about pulling them. The Belmonts have been riding them too hard and not making sure they drink. But why would they use Tara's electrolytes instead of their own?"

Laurie explained about the Arabian race contest. "If they think those electrolytes are what's making Hawk so fast, they might try them. All of them are out to win at any price."

That got everyone on their feet, protesting. "This is exactly what the sport is *not* about!"

"That's why we don't have money prizes."

"People are supposed to do these races for the love of it!"

Janet looked grim. "I wish I'd pulled those horses," she said. "They could be in trouble, anywhere on the trail. We can't chase after them in trucks. We need horses, but nobody's come in yet."

"There are a few spare horses at base camp," Laurie pointed out. "It'll just take me ten or fifteen minutes to drive back."

"And another fifteen at least to get the horses loaded, and then drive back here, and then ride in." Janet wiped the sweat off her forehead. "I'm afraid we may be too late if they've given them those electrolytes. But, right now, it's our only shot."

She motioned to one of the volunteers. "Cindy, you go with Mrs. Sandersen and help her bring up some horses. I'll get an emergency kit ready and stay put, in case Omar and Ali Baba turn up here."

Riding through dense pines, Becky felt the sharp sting of a dead branch flick across her cheek. She was tired to her bones—weary in every muscle—but the thought of Omar stretched on the ground in that gloomy thicket spurred her on.

She finally burst out of the dense pine plantation into the easier going of the new forest.

Another twenty minutes of hard riding brought her out on the gravel road that led to the third vet check.

Becky urged Shadow forward. "Come on, girl, we've got to fly!"

The paint mare snorted, tossed her head and galloped downhill toward the grassy field where the third vet check was set up.

To Becky's enormous relief, the vet's truck was parked beside her small trailer. People were gathered around, waiting for the first riders to come in. Becky loped Shadow across the field and pulled up to a row of shocked faces.

"What have you done to yourself?" Janet grabbed Shadow's bridle.

"What?" They were staring at her face. Her hand flew up to touch something sticky. Blood?

"Dead branch caught my cheek," she gasped.

"Doesn't matter. Listen! Omar, Graham Belmont's horse, has had some kind of seizure. Rob's with him."

They were still staring at her.

"Get off your horse," Janet insisted. "Let me see your face. Great heavens, girl, you need stitches. Look at your shirt!"

Becky looked down. The top of her T-shirt, which she'd thought was just sweaty, was totally soaked in blood. Hers!

She slipped off Shadow, feeling faint.

"We've got to get help for Omar," she mumbled. "I don't know what's wrong with him."

"Acute metabolic distress, most likely," Janet said grimly, leading Becky by the hand into the trailer. "Your mother's gone to get some horses so we can look for him and Ali Baba. We think they might have been given Tara's electrolytes. In fact, from your description, I'm sure that's the problem."

"Are you serious?"

"I hope not, but it looks that way." The whole time she was talking, Janet had been swabbing Becky's cheek with distilled water. "I don't have a fine enough needle to sew you up."

Becky smiled weakly. "Glad to hear it." Her cheek was starting to sting like fury.

"But we can't let you go on bleeding like this." Janet reached for a metal box. "I'm going to use tape and do butterfly stitches. Are you okay?"

"Go ahead, Doc," Becky gulped. "How long till Mom gets back?"

"Not long. In the meantime, some of the lead horses should be here soon."

As Janet was working on her cheek, there was the roar of an engine outside.

"Hold still!" Janet ordered as Becky's head jerked up.

"That sounds like an ATV." Becky gripped Janet's arm. "We don't have to wait for horses. That four-wheeler could get us to Rob and Omar."

"Maybe." Janet forced Becky's hand down. "But first I'm going to finish putting you back together. Keep still and let me do my job!"

Becky could remember when all she wanted in the world was an all-terrain vehicle. That had been two years ago, when she was thirteen and would rather have been riding an ATV than a horse. Now, the ATV she was riding just seemed like a noisy machine that tore up good horse trails.

But it would take them where no truck could go. Bouncing along behind Janet, Becky was relieved to be in motion, to be doing something.

The ATV owner had been happy to lend his machine to a good cause. "She's got lots of speed," he said proudly. "Just bring her back in one piece." He was a tall young man in a helmet and a suit thick with road dust.

"Keep your head down!" Janet yelled as they entered the thickly grown pine forest. "I don't want to bandage up any more gashes in your face."

Becky suddenly remembered the soft touch on the cheek Rob had given her—on the same cheek she'd cut. It was throbbing with pain now, but she knew she'd remember the touch longer than the swipe of the pine branch. It wasn't much, but from Rob it meant a lot.

"There he is!" Becky pointed ahead.

Janet slowed the ATV down as they got close, afraid of spooking the horses with the motor's roar.

When Janet shut off the engine, the silence rang in Becky's ears. There was only the terrible sound of Omar's ragged breathing.

Rob was cradling Omar's head in his lap. "He's bad," he muttered without taking his eyes off the suffering horse.

Janet dropped to her knees with her stethoscope and felt his heart. She shook her head.

When Janet opened her bag, Becky saw the medication she'd brought for a humane killing if Omar could not be saved. As she was packing it, she'd warned Becky, "I'll do everything I can for him, but I won't let him suffer."

Now she filled a large syringe and plunged it into Omar's neck.

Was this the lethal injection? Becky sucked in her breath.

Janet looked up at her. "I'm trying a dose of electrolytes first. It will either work fast or not at all."

Becky waited, breathless. The big dark horse lay so still —it seemed hopeless.

Janet gave another small shake of her head. "Take Windy away," she said quietly to Becky. "We don't want her freaking out."

Feeling a sob in her throat, Becky undid Windy's rope and led her off into the trees. She wanted to run, but there was no way to move quickly through the snarled branches.

Windy whickered unhappily, picking up her sad vibrations. Steeling herself, Becky waited for the moment when Omar's ragged breathing would stop forever.

CHAPTER 17

MIRACLE SHOT

Becky stood with Windy's bridle firmly gripped in her hand. The mare threw her head up and quivered down the length of her body. It was as though she could smell death close by in that tangled grove of trees.

"It's all right," Becky soothed her with a quiet voice. "Janet knows what she's doing. There's nothing to be frightened of. It will be over soon."

She said the words, but inside, her weary brain was whirling and her stomach flip-flopped.

Growing up on ranches, Becky had seen calves die at birth, chickens slaughtered for food and horses put down because of injuries or killed in accidents. She remembered Old Pie, a Mustang Mountain horse who died when a cougar leaped on him from a ledge, and Copper, a friend's horse swept away in the Cauldron River rapids. Death was part of life with animals, even with the horses you loved. She leaned her head against Windy's mane. "But we're still scared, aren't we?" she whispered.

Windy's head bobbed up and down. Then she gave an eager little whinny, perked up her ears and pawed the ground.

"What?" Becky straightened. What did Windy see? What did she hear?

Now she could hear it, too. The sound of voices, of a horse blowing, of movement in the trees.

"Becky!" she heard Rob shout. "Come here. Come quick!"

"Let's go, Windy!" Dragging the mare behind her, Becky dived under branches, clambered over tree trunks.

She could hardly believe the sight that met her in the trampled clearing. There was Omar, standing like a proud Arabian statue. He was scraped and bleeding, but his eyes were bright, his ears up and his muscles no longer twitched.

"What happened?" Becky could hardly breathe.

Janet shook her head, grinning. "Balance the electrolytes —potassium, sodium, calcium and the others—and bingo! The horse comes back to life." She grew serious. "In other words, we got here in time to give him that injection. *Just* in time."

"It's like a miracle." Becky let out her breath.

"Thanks to you." Rob beamed at Janet. "I was never so glad in my life as when I heard that ATV."

Janet had already set to work cleaning and mending Omar's puncture wounds and scrapes. "He looks like a piece of fine furniture that got pitched downstairs," she sighed. "This perfect shiny hide is going to have some scars."

Becky put her hand up to her own face. "Will I scar?"

"You?" Rob suddenly stared at her in horror, noticing the bandage and the bloody T-shirt for the first time. "Holy cow! What happened?"

"A tree branch got me. I guess my perfect hide won't ever be the same again, either." Becky tried to grin, but it hurt.

"I could kill Graham Belmont," Rob said through gritted teeth. "Janet told me that he's the cause of all this. Tara was right about him."

Becky glanced at him quickly. She'd forgotten for a while about Tara. But Rob hadn't.

"Yes," she said. "I guess this means Tara wins. She'll be off to race Hawk across the desert."

Janet made a rude noise, bending over Omar's cut hock. "I wish I'd known about their ridiculous Arabian race," she muttered. "Once I get this fellow fixed up, we have to find Ali Baba and hope we're not too late to save *him*."

"You go ahead on the four-wheeler," Becky suggested. "Rob can walk Omar to the vet check."

"All right." Janet put her supplies back in her bag. "Go slow. Omar still needs to take it easy."

She hopped on the ATV and drove away slowly. But

as soon as she disappeared into the dense woods, Rob and Becky heard the engine roar into full power, then fade in the distance.

As the sound died away, Becky hoisted herself wearily into Windy's saddle.

"What are you doing?" Rob's eyes narrowed. "I thought we were walking the horses back."

Becky sighed. "You don't need me to take Omar back. I know I should probably stay and look for Ali Baba, but there'll be lots of other people to help. I made a promise to myself, and my mom. I'm going to complete the race like I said I would. I'm going to finish riding this shortcut, find the right trail and ride the rest of the Wildflower 50."

"Are you nuts?" Rob gaped at her. "I can't believe you're even thinking of going on. Your face!"

Becky shook her head. "Don't argue with me, Rob. A little scratch on my cheek isn't going to stop me."

"You call that a little scratch!" Rob shook his head. "You're the most pig-headed person I've ever known. I'm not going to argue with you because it would be no use. I'll just say one more time that this is dangerous and stupid, and your mother would not want you heading off by yourself in this state."

"Maybe not," Becky agreed, "but I'm going to do it. Good luck, Rob."

Rob watched her turn Windy slowly around and head down the shortcut, ducking low under the dead branches. "Come on, Omar." He clucked the big bay horse forward. "When she makes up her mind, there's no stopping her. She thinks her cousin Alison is stubborn? Ha! Becky's the one with cement for brains. I just hope she knows what she's doing."

Not far from the shortcut, Tara was lost in a maze of ATV trails.

She pulled Hawk to a stop. "We've come a long way and we haven't seen a white flag in ages," she said out loud. "I must have made a wrong turn. We'll have to go back."

Wheeling Hawk around, Tara headed back the way they'd come. But the track they were on soon met another. Which way now? Left or right? Or straight ahead?

They turned left. Tara searched for signs of horses, hoofprints, horse manure, white flags, anything that would show she'd made the right choice.

Nothing. Should she go back?

Tara tried to fight off the clouds of confusion that filled her brain. "Drink!" she heard Becky's command, so she reached in her pack for a water bottle, opened it with fumbling fingers and took a big gulp.

Instantly, a wave of nausea struck. She leaned forward, groaning, over Hawk's neck. "Ugh! Can't drink. Sick."

Not drinking, riding hard, not eating—it had all caught up to her. In despair, she flung the bottle of water into the trees.

"Got to find the trail," she mumbled, looking help-lessly around. "C'mon, Hawk, find the other horses." She tried to remember what Becky had said about not getting lost in the wilderness, something about the sun, and the mountain—but it was all a blur in her head.

"I just need to lie down for a while... let my head clear," she sighed, sliding off Hawk's back. The idea of being lost was so terrifying that she curled into a ball of misery, hugging her knees. When she felt better, she'd find her way back to the ride trail.

Hawk, his reins dangling, looked down on Tara's still body. He lowered his head and sniffed her gently, then walked away, looking for grass to munch, water to drink.

CHAPTER 18

LOST IN A MAZE

Tara lifted her head and looked around.

Hawk was gone. How much time had passed, she wasn't sure.

Slowly, through a fogged brain, the full misery of her situation sunk in. She was lost in a maze of ATV trails— far from the ride route, without her horse. No one would find her here.

The small clearing was empty. No sound except the wailing of the wind through the trees. A wave of cold fear swept through her. She got to her feet, howling.

"Hawk! Hawk," she sobbed, stumbling forward. She would die in this terrible place, and the animals would devour her body. She would never see Hawk again, never ride him across the desert.

The wind seemed to trick her, calling her name. The sound came and went with the sighing of the trees. She was alone.

She stumbled again and, this time, went down hard, wrenching her ankle.

Tara pulled herself up on a fallen log and loosened her shoe. The pain was numbed by the fog in her brain—it was so hard to think—but one thing was sure. If she'd needed help before, she needed it more desperately now.

A cool afternoon wind had come up. It blew from the northwest, making Becky's tired muscles shiver. She ached with weariness, but rode on. This was her first endurance race, and she wasn't going to have an "incomplete" on Windy's record. "To finish is to win"—wasn't that the motto of endurance riders? Well, she was going to finish.

She knew Rob didn't understand. What had he called her? Pig-headed—that was it. "I'm not pig-headed," she told Windy. "Just determined. What's wrong with that? If a guy is determined, they say he's strong and tough. But *girls* just get called stubborn!"

Windy bobbed her head as if she understood. "You're tough, too." Becky bent down to pat her neck. As they forced their way through the thick tangle of trees, Becky went over their route in her mind.

First to the creek so Windy could drink. Then on to

the fork where she'd made the wrong turn, over the trail to the second vet check, then the third, and finally the last part of the ride to home base.

Becky glanced at her watch. It would be very late by the time she reached the end. They had to make it within the twelve-hour time limit set for the Wildflower 50. It would take all her determination, pig-headedness, or whatever you wanted to call it, to get there.

The wind blew through the treetops, sighing and moaning.

A few minutes later, she walked Windy down the rock-strewn bank of the dry stream. The hole they had dug with their hands was full of clear water. Becky slipped from Windy's back with a grateful sigh. "Have a good long drink," she told the mare. "We made it through the hardest part."

She yanked out her own water bottle and took a long pull while she watched Windy make her way over the rounded stones.

Becky sucked in her breath. Now that they were out in the open, she could see that Windy's hide was cut and scraped. She was hurt and tired, and there was a deep scratch on the mare's forehead.

"The two of us are a mess, and we still have a really long way to go." Becky sighed. "What do you think? Am I asking too much?" She made her way over to the mare.

At that moment, Windy lifted her head and gave a soft neigh. Her ears pricked forward.

"What is it? What do you hear?" At first, all Becky

could hear was the wind. Then her ears caught the sound. The unmistakable clop of a horse's hoofs coming upstream over the rocks.

Hawk appeared around a bend in the creek.

Windy gave a louder welcoming neigh, and Hawk answered with a joyful whinny. He came forward to greet Windy, reins dangling. The two horses met nose to nose, then Hawk lowered his muzzle into the waterhole to drink.

"Hawk!" Becky gasped. "Where's Tara?"

She waited long moments for Tara to come walking up the stream, then bellowed, "Tara! Where are you?" The north wind blew her words back in her face. "Tara! Can you hear me?"

No answer. That stupid, ignorant idiot girl had somehow let her horse wander off. How Hawk had managed not to break a leg with his reins hanging loose like that she didn't know.

"If I go look for Tara, I'll lose more time." Becky cursed out loud. "But I have to look for her. She must be in major trouble."

She started off up the creek bed, leading Windy and Hawk. It was slow picking their way over the rounded stones and not safe for the horses, especially Hawk, with his slender leg bones. But the banks of the stream were too thick with trees to walk beside it. Somewhere, there would be a break in the trees, a path that Hawk must have taken to reach the creek.

Meanwhile, at the third vet check, Laurie Sandersen looked up at Rob with a shake of her head.

"You mean that after all that—riding back on Shadow to get help, tearing her cheek on a tree branch, helping with Omar—Becky *still* insisted on finishing the race? I wish you hadn't let her go, Rob. She had so far to ride—"

"I'm sorry." Rob looked sheepish. "I should have tied her to a pine tree."

That made Laurie grin. "I know. Changing Becky's mind, once it's made up, is like tryin' to stop a tornado." Her face grew serious. "I just hope she's all right, and Windy, too."

"Me, too. If anything happened to Becky …" Rob gulped. It was agony, thinking of her alone out there on a mountain trail, with the afternoon getting late.

Laurie interrupted his thoughts. "And where's Tara? She should have been here almost an hour ago. That girl's so inexperienced—who knows what kind of trouble she's in."

After ten minutes of careful searching along the stream bed, Becky found the break in the trees she'd been looking for.

"It's an ATV track!" she breathed in surprise, noting the deep ruts in the stream bank. "If Tara was on this track, she must have *really* got off trail."

She mounted Windy in one swift motion. "Let's go," she clucked to Hawk, holding his reins so he would follow.

The ATV track wound through the woods, up a long rise, then dove steeply downhill. Here, Becky could clearly see the damage the machines had done, chewing up the slope, creating channels for water to erode the mountainside, making the slope even steeper.

From the top, she could see straight down into a small clearing. A drooping figure was slumped on a fallen log. Tara! For one split second, Becky allowed herself to feel glad to see her in such misery—not proud, not boastful, not flaunting her beauty like some haughty thoroughbred. Just a sad, lost girl, alone on a log.

"Can't just leave her there. Come on, let's go, guys."

The hillside was too steep and deeply rutted to ride. Becky slipped off Windy's back and looped her reins safely around her saddle. "Tara!" she shouted. "We're coming." She started down, slipping and sliding, still holding Hawk's reins. Windy she trusted not to run off.

But Windy, not used to such unnatural footing, caught her left foreleg in one of the ruts and almost fell. Becky sucked in her breath, but Windy recovered and hurtled down the hill to Tara.

By the time Becky and Hawk reached the bottom, Tara had risen to her feet and thrown both arms around Windy's neck.

"You found me!" she sobbed, burying her blond head in Windy's chestnut mane. She looked up at Becky and wiped her teary eyes with a limp hand. "But I don't understand," she marveled. "How did you and Windy get here? I thought you were finishing the race."

"I *was* finishing the race, riding the shortcut—" Becky explained. "That's where I found Hawk. He was up at the creek—"

She stepped forward and stroked Windy's velvety nose. "Are you all right, girl? That was quite a dash." Windy shifted her weight and Becky saw she was favoring her right foreleg. The hurtle down the hill had been costly.

Tara slumped back to the ground. "So, you weren't looking for me. You just found Hawk by accident." Her voice rose to a wail. "Are you going back to the shortcut? Are you going to leave me here? I'll never find my way out of these awful ATV trails. They all look the same, and they twist around … and I've sprained my ankle."

"I don't know." Becky wanted desperately to go on, but Tara seemed so helpless—even if she deserved it, it wouldn't be right to leave her here. She ran a hand down Windy's sweaty neck. "I guess not. I'll take you as far as the ride trail. Then I have to go back. I promised myself I'd finish the race!"

"Sure, you'll finish. But for me, the race is over." Tara sank to the ground. "Hawk and I have lost everything."

Becky snorted in disgust. "You're still alive, aren't you? You're lucky, and so is Hawk, that he didn't break a leg. How could you let him go like that, with his reins dragging?"

"I felt so dizzy—so sick." Tara fluttered her hands. "I got off, and then I lay down for just a minute, because I was too weak to stand."

"Of course you were!" Becky glared down at her. "You haven't eaten enough or drunk enough all day. You're dehydrated, that's all that's wrong with you. Here!" She dug a water bottle out of Windy's pack and shoved it at Tara. "Drink! And let me have a look at that ankle."

CHAPTER 19

TOUGH DECISION

"Take a small sip—a very small sip, and then another, till you stop feeling dizzy," Becky insisted.

Tara shrugged in disbelief, but sipped at the water with a sour expression. The haze of confusion in her brain began to disappear. She saw Becky clearly.

"You look horrible!" She stared at her bandaged cheek and bloody shirt. "What happened?"

"Caught my cheek on a branch. It bled all over me before I could get to a bandage... Never mind that. Keep drinking."

A few minutes later, Tara managed a wan smile. "You were right. I feel better." After a couple of bites of a power bar, the color was back in her face. She smiled sheepishly at Becky. "Next time, I'll know to eat."

Becky turned her attention to Tara's ankle. "That ankle needs some pressure to keep the swelling down. I've got a tensor bandage somewhere in here." Becky dug the roll of elastic bandage out of her pack and wrapped it carefully around Tara's foot and ankle.

"It doesn't look too serious." She handed Tara her sock. "You should be able to ride."

"You know all this useful stuff…" Tara struggled to pull her sock on over the bandage.

"It's part of what you learn when you train for endurance." Becky shrugged. "Mom's always nagging at me about what to pack, and what to eat, and how many times to drink…"

"I wish I had a mother like yours," Tara sighed.

"Yeah, I'm lucky." By now, she thought, her mother would be waiting for her at the third vet check. It would be such a long ride to get there, once she had guided Tara back to the ride trail. The weary miles spun out in Becky's brain.

"Let's go," she told Tara.

"I hope we can find our way," Tara groaned. "I tried—"

"Keep the sun over your left shoulder." Becky helped Tara onto Hawk, then climbed into Windy's saddle.

They rode in silence. I haven't heard one word of thanks, Becky thought, not one word of gratitude for finding Hawk, or saving Tara's miserable hide again or helping her out of this tangle of trails. Personality plus— that's Tara!

But as they worked their way through the maze of

trails, Becky soon forgot to be grumpy about Tara. She had a bigger problem.

Something was wrong with Windy's stride. It wasn't really a limp, but it could easily develop into one if that right leg was stressed any further. To save the mare's leg, Becky hopped off Windy at the worst spots on the ATV trail, where the soil was so deeply churned and rutted that it was dangerous for any horse.

At last they rode out onto the wider, softer ride trail. It was plainly marked with the prints of many horses.

"You'll be fine now. Head that way." Becky pointed in the direction of the third vet check. "And for Pete's sake, watch for the ride ribbons."

"You're really going to leave me?" Tara cried.

"I have to. Good luck."

"I have to do this," Becky repeated to herself as she rode away from Tara. "I have to finish the Wildflower 50."

In the next moment, Windy tripped on a tree root in the trail.

Close one! Becky slid from her saddle and walked to Windy's head.

"How're you doing?" she asked softly. "You all right?"

Windy's warm brown eyes blinked. She raised her head to rest her soft nose on Becky's stomach.

Becky could see Windy's lip droop. The mare's whole posture screamed fatigue. "If I asked, you'd keep going if it killed you." Becky whispered. "Even though your leg hurts, and you're scraped and bruised and beat up." Tears spurted to her own eyes. "You'd do it, if I asked."

She turned Windy on the trail, climbed wearily back in the saddle and set off back the way she'd come. "Tara, wait!" she shouted.

When she caught up, Tara looked pitifully glad to see her, but confused. "I thought you were going back to ride the trail..."

"Endurance is all about looking after my horse," Becky sighed. "Windy's tired and getting lame. It's the end of the race for us, too."

A smile brightened Tara's lean face. "I'm glad I'm not the only one. And I'm glad you're here to help us stay on the trail. It'll be so much easier for me."

For you! Becky thought bitterly. Everything's for you, isn't it?

She had never felt so weary and defeated in her entire life.

Laurie was looking down the tunnel of trees at the trail's end. She and Rob had been waiting at the third vet station for hours, it seemed. Almost all the riders had been through. The ones who'd met up with Janet on the trail and helped look for Ali Baba were still at the vet check. Others were just waiting for their hold time to end.

"Do you think I should go looking for Becky. Or...

Tara?" Rob asked. "I've still got Shadow, and she's fairly fresh. Laurie? What's the matter?"

Laurie was staring at the trail. "You don't need to go looking for anybody. Here they come. Both of them— together again!"

She hurried forward. "Rob, can you see to Hawk?" she called over her shoulder.

Rob paused. Tara was riding in front, slumped in Hawk's saddle. Becky was leading Windy, who seemed to be favoring one leg. Both of them looked totally miserable.

Rob caught at Laurie's arm. "If you don't mind, I'd like to give Becky a hand with Windy."

Laurie began to shake her head, then saw the look on Rob's face. "You go ahead." Laurie gave him a quick nod. "I'm sure it's you Becky wants to see."

"Rob!" Tara cried piteously. "Help me…" She slid from her saddle and stood on one foot, holding out the reins as Rob ran forward.

To her shock, he strode right past her, went to Becky and threw his arm around her shoulders.

"I'm so glad to see you!" He gazed at her scratched, bandaged face and her bloody T-shirt. When she yanked off her helmet, her fair hair was snarled and matted. Still she made his heart thump.

He swallowed hard. "Where? How? Why did you end up with Tara?"

"It's a long story." Becky took a deep breath, feeling the wonderful warmth of Rob's arm close around her. As they walked to the cooling station leading Windy, she explained. "I found Hawk, running loose with his reins dangling, then Tara, collapsed in a clearing all by herself."

"Hawk was loose?" Rob asked. "How did that happen?"

"Tara was totally dehydrated from not eating or drinking all day—and she let Hawk wander off." Becky sighed. "I'm glad I found them before anything really bad happened, but the thing is, Rob, I didn't finish the race. I didn't complete the Wildflower."

Her eyes filled with tears. Rob pulled a sponge out of his pocket and dabbed at them.

"Rob! That's a horse sponge."

"I know. I just can't stand to see you cry. Forget about the race. You're here, and you're safe."

They reached the water tanks. "We should get Windy's saddle off," Becky said. Rob still had his arm around her.

"I know." Rob gently touched her bandaged cheek. "Wait. I want to—I guess I can't kiss you on the cheek, can I?"

"It's a bit sore." Becky looked up at him.

"Then I'll have to do this. I've been wanting to, all summer." Still holding Windy's reins, Rob drew her close and kissed her lips.

Becky felt dizzy, whether from exhaustion, dehydration or the thrill of his kiss, it didn't matter. She kissed him back and felt the green dragon of jealousy shrink to a small lizard, then skitter away.

Tara looked up, scowling. She had let Laurie cool Hawk off while she rewound her bandage. "Look at that!" Tara cried. "Ha! I *knew* he was her boyfriend."

Laurie turned in time to see Becky and Rob pull apart, still gazing into each other's eyes. "That's their business," Laurie told Tara firmly. "Let's work on your horse."

"Well, my mother would have something to say if somebody kissed *me* right out in the open, where everybody can see," muttered Tara. "She'd never allow me to do anything like that!"

CHAPTER 20

FINAL RUN

"Rob, isn't that Ali Baba?" Becky recognized the bay Arabian standing calmly in the center of a group of people at the third vet check. "What a relief! I was so afraid they'd find him too late." They had finished cooling the horses and were grazing them in the shade.

"What do you mean 'too late'?" Tara gave her an astonished glance. "I met Gwendolyn Belmont on the trail—before I got lost. She was babbling about getting thrown off Ali Baba. And where's Omar?"

"He had a close call—they probably trailered him back to base camp." Becky quickly explained about the stolen electrolytes and Janet's rescue of Omar in the bush. "I'm sorry," she apologized to Tara. "We all thought you were exaggerating about the Belmonts."

"How could I?" Tara tossed her head. "They're so awful. I'm not surprised they would try a trick like that. Poor horses!" She paused, struck with a terrible thought. "I could have given those electrolytes to Hawk! I could have killed him."

Tara suddenly had another thought. It lit up her face like a Christmas light. "Does this mean that neither Omar or Ali Baba can complete the race? Are they out of it?"

Laurie was tending to Windy's leg, wrapping it with ice from the cooler and a bandage.

She glanced at Tara. "Afraid so. You and the Belmonts had no business usin' the Wildflower 50 for your own purposes."

"It was the toughest endurance test we could find around here." Tara drew herself up straight, flinging back her ponytail. "Just tell me. Is Hawk fit to go on?"

"I think so." Laurie studied the big Arabian. "But you'll have to pass the vet check first."

"We're disqualified, anyway," Becky shot in. "Don't forget that."

"You know I don't care about the rules. As long as Hawk finishes the race and the other two don't, we win."

"But even if Hawk is okay, are *you* fit to go on?" Laurie looked at her critically. "Becky says you weren't feeling too well when she found you, and I'm not sure you can ride with that ankle."

"I just needed to balance my own electrolytes." Tara's eyes sparkled. "I feel fine now, and my ankle's not sore enough to keep me out of this race."

"Well, the vet's still set up over there." Laurie pointed. "Why don't you go and get Hawk checked out?"

"I will." Tara limped off with Hawk toward the vet station.

"It's like she's electrified." Becky ran her fingers through her sweaty hair, watching Tara go. "She's got guts, you have to give her that."

"Sometimes it takes more guts to know when to quit," Laurie said quietly. "I'm very proud of you, Becky. You thought about Windy first. That's something worth remembering."

"But I didn't finish," Becky mourned. "I'll never forget that."

"There's Graham Belmont," said Rob a few minutes later. He pointed to a man propped up in a chair. "Doesn't look too happy."

"Serves him right," Becky muttered under her breath.

When Janet had finished checking the last horse, she came over to check on Windy.

"You're doing the right thing, icing Windy's leg," she told Laurie. "If she takes it easy, your mare should be fine." She turned to Rob. "Can you give me a hand to get Graham Belmont into Laurie's truck? It looks like he has a broken rib or two from his tumble off Omar. We should get him to the hospital."

Rob and Becky walked with her and Laurie to Graham's

folding green chair. "Be careful." He winced as Rob tried to lift him. "Every move is torture!"

"Where did they find him?" Becky asked her mother, shooting a disgusted glance at Graham.

"Ali Baba was standing over him not far off the trail. After throwing Gwendolyn and bolting, I guess Ali Baba wandered back to stay by his side."

Which was a lot more than he deserved, Becky thought. How could anyone hurt such brave, faithful horses? "How is Ali Baba now?"

"He was fine once Janet gave him a shot. He wasn't as bad off as Omar."

"Can you get me my waist pack from the trailer, somebody?" Graham called peevishly. "I've got some painkiller in there and I'm going to need it."

"I'll get it." Becky found the canvas pack in the vets' trailer and unzipped it, looking for the painkiller.

"Galloping grasshoppers! Look at that," she gasped in surprise as something red drifted to the floor.

It was a red ribbon.

She walked over to Graham Belmont. "Does this look familiar, Mr. Belmont?"

His face twitched. "Where did you find that?"

"Tied to a tree, where I took a wrong turn." Becky waved the ribbon in his face.

"But I removed it! It's in my—" Graham stopped as he realized what he was saying. His face grew red. He tried to snatch the ribbon from Becky, but his broken ribs stopped him with a gasp.

"Why did you do it?" Becky demanded. "Why didn't you try to beat Hawk and Tara in a fair race? You and your sister are experienced riders. Tara's just a beginner."

"We—we wanted to be sure." Graham lowered his eyes. "She has a good horse."

Becky wanted to strangle him with his own ribbon. "You ruined the race for both of us!" she yelled. "And your cheating almost killed Omar."

"It's all right." Laurie took her hand. "It's time to let it go, Becky."

"All right." Becky shoved the ribbon in her pocket. "But you all saw it, didn't you?" Her eyes swept her mother, Rob and Janet. "You heard what he said. He threw us off trail, on purpose!"

"We heard." Janet glared at Graham Belmont. "I hope you've learned something today, Mr. Belmont." She put his arm over her shoulders and started to walk him toward the truck. "Sometimes winning at any cost isn't worth the price!"

On the last leg of the Wildflower 50, Tara slowed Hawk's pace. When the hills were steep, she got off to walk beside him, even though her ankle throbbed with pain. He was running well on the flat, and by the end of the race, she'd overtaken two other stragglers. The three sped up as the base camp came into view.

"I should run the final dash beside you," Tara panted,

"but I've got a sore ankle and I know you want to gallop with those other horses. We may be the last three in the race, but you can beat them!"

"Go!" Tara gave him the signal. "Fly, my Hawk!"

Hawk surged forward. The three horses pounded up the hill toward the small group of people waiting—the timekeeper, the crews, her mother in her long skirt!

A nose ahead of the other two, Hawk crossed the finish line.

"We did it!" Tara's face shone with satisfaction. She threw herself off his back. Hawk was breathing hard, nostrils extended, body glistening with sweat.

Tara's mother hurried forward with a bucket, slopping water.

"That was thrilling, dear," she gasped. "You won!"

"We were the last three horses in the race, mother." Tara whipped off her helmet. "It doesn't count, but it sure was fun."

She looked around the grassy field. "Where's my crew?"

"They're at base camp with Becky and Windy." Her mother handed her a sponge. "I guess I'm your crew, dear. Shouldn't we be getting Hawk ready for his vet check?"

Tara stared at her mother. How did she know stuff like that?

"I guess we can do it ourselves!" she exclaimed. "Here, give me that bucket."

"You have a remarkable horse," said George, the other veterinarian, after a careful inspection of Hawk. It was the final vet check, an hour after Tara had logged in.

He straightened up to smile at her. "No sign of damage to the legs, and he's nearly as sound as when he started. Congratulations."

"But we didn't win." Tara stroked Hawk's neck. "Everybody else was ahead of us."

"No, but that was a great finish." The vet grinned. "Three horses, almost neck and neck, galloping uphill, at the end of a fifty-mile race." He took off his ball cap and scratched his head. "I've been vetting for endurance races for a lot of years, and I'm telling you, you don't see that every day."

"Listen to that, darling!" Tara's mother, standing with clasped hands, cried. "Hawk is a *remarkable* horse."

As Tara limped away from the vet check leading Hawk, a short man in a dark suit hurried to walk beside her.

"I am Mr. Abrahim," he announced, holding out his hand.

Tara shook it. "The sheik's agent?"

"The same," he said politely. "I hope you have not injured yourself too badly." He nodded at her bandaged ankle.

"It's just a sprain—I'll be fine." Tara held her breath. What was he going to say about the race?

"I see no sign of the owners of Ali Baba and Omar. What can you tell me of them? Are they here?"

Tara gulped. What should she tell him? That the Gee-Gees cheated, stole electrolytes, poisoned their horses? Mr. Abrahim would probably find out soon enough—gossip spread quickly in the horse world.

"You'll have to ask the Belmonts." Tara threw back her head. "I think they may have had bad luck on the trail. I'm not sure where they are now." That was the truth, at least.

"Well," the agent beamed, "I cannot say for certain, but it seems that you and Hawk will be the guests of my employer this winter. Hawk has run a splendid race, according to the veterinarian. And the way he raced those horses at the end and beat them—what spirit!"

"Did you hear that, Hawk?" Tara laughed. "We're going to Arabia!"

CHAPTER 21

Awards

The awards ceremony for the Wildflower 50 was held at twilight.

All the riders, crew and ride volunteers sat in a semi-circle in front of the trailer at the base camp. On a table were the ribbons for the top ten riders and the coveted Best Condition award for the horse judged to be in the best shape at the end of the race.

Becky sat on the ground between her mother and Rob. On his other side was Tara, her bandaged ankle stretched out in front of her. Eva was beside her on a lawn chair.

Her mother had presented Becky with an official Wildflower 50 T-shirt to take the place of her bloody one. She looked down at the spray of wildflowers across a mountain scene on the front, listening with half an ear to the announcements.

"And the winner of the novice class is Tara Kosaric on Hawk!"

Tara let out a squeal of surprise and delight. She hopped on her good leg to claim her ribbon, ponytail dancing.

"Tara and I were the *only* novice riders," Becky grumbled to Rob. "But look at her, you'd think she'd won the Nobel Prize."

Her mother squeezed her hand. "You may ride thousands of miles in endurance races, darlin', but I'll bet you'll always remember this race you didn't win."

"Didn't even complete," Becky groaned.

Just then, there was a disturbance in the crowd on the other side, and Gregory Belmont stood awkwardly from his chair. "I think Miss Kosaric should be disqualified," he called out. "I know for a fact that she left the official route during the second part of the ride and took a shortcut."

There was silence while everybody looked at Tara. Her excited face crumpled into a frown. "You…" she started.

Becky clambered to her feet. "Wait a minute," she called. "I have something to say. I found this in Graham Belmont's waist pack this afternoon." She pulled the red silk ribbon from her pocket. "Tara took the wrong trail, and so did I, because Graham tied this to a tree to confuse us. After we passed, he untied it. He admitted it." She glared at Gregory. "In front of witnesses."

There were gasps of indignation from the group.

"As for the shortcut," she went on, "it wasn't an easy path, as you can see from my face. So I don't think Tara should be disqualified." She paused. "That's all."

There was clapping and shouts of "No disqualification."

"We'll have to take a few minutes to think about this and make a decision," the ride manager announced.

Becky was struck by the look on Tara's face—confusion, shame and delight, all mixed together. There might even have been a touch of gratitude in there, Becky thought with a grin.

"It's so amazing you found the ribbon!" Tara exclaimed. "You were right all along. You *did* see a red ribbon on the tree where we turned. Those terrible Gee-Gees sent us on the wrong route."

"I think they got what they deserved," Becky said. "Omar almost died, and Graham will be a long time recovering."

"How is Ali Baba?" Tara asked.

"Better," Becky told her. "Gwendolyn told me she didn't trust her brothers and wouldn't give Ali Baba the double dose they gave Omar."

Tara laughed. "Poor old Gwendolyn. How would you like to have two brothers like Graham and Gregory? Mine are bad enough." She held up her ribbon proudly. "But they're going to be nicer to Hawk and me when they see this, and when I get to go to Arabia."

She looked down at Rob, batting her long eyelashes. "If you're not doing anything over the Christmas break,

I'd like you to come with Mother and me and Hawk to the race in the desert. We could use your help."

"Yes," Eva nodded, smiling. "We would be happy to pay your way."

Becky held her breath. What an offer! The green dragon threatened to rear its ugly head again, but Becky looked Rob square in the face. "You should go, Rob. It would be the trip of a lifetime."

Rob's face broke into a broad smile. "Thank you, Tara, Mrs. Kosaric. I appreciate your offer, but I'm afraid I can't go. I have to look after our ranch at Horner Creek, and have Christmas with my sister, Sara." He paused. "And maybe Becky, if she can make it down from Mustang Mountain for a few days."

"Oh, well. It was worth a try." Tara turned and whispered to Becky. "He's your boyfriend, like I said."

Just then, there was a shout from the front of the group. "If we could have your attention—under the unusual circumstances, the ride committee feels it would be proper to let Tara Kosaric keep her novice ribbon."

There were loud cheers. Tara hugged her mother and flopped back on the grass with a satisfied smirk.

"Now, if you could just pay attention for a few more moments, we have other awards to give out."

Becky sat down, feeling the warmth of Rob's closeness. As the rest of the awards were read out, her mind drifted off again. She gazed around at the horses tied to trailers or in pens, peacefully eating, resting. At the other riders, trying to clap while balancing plates of cake on their laps, or running forward to collect their ribbons in their blue Wildflower 50 T-shirts. How could they still run after everything they'd done that day?

The pink glow was fading over the mountains. Soon, they'd light the bonfire. They'd sit around it, telling stories about their rides and their horses. Becky thought about how lonely she'd be when all this was over and she was back at Mustang Mountain by herself.

Tomorrow. When Rob was gone.

Suddenly her mother nudged her arm. "Listen!"

"... not every year we give out this special award," the ride manager was saying. "It's for a rider who best exemplifies the spirit of our sport. This year," he paused, "we are proud to present this award to Becky Sandersen, who reminded us what endurance racing is all about."

Stunned, Becky stood on shaky legs and ran forward to collect a small bronze statue of an endurance horse and rider. Rob and her mother beamed and clapped. Even Tara was smiling.

Before the bonfire, Tara limped over to the Sandersens' trailer to say goodbye to Becky.

"Mother wants to get back to Calgary and sleep in her own bed," Tara sighed. "She says she's tired of roughing it. So—I guess we have to go."

The lights were on and she stood in the pool of light from the trailer door, looking just as she had when she'd come to ask them to help find Hawk the night before.

But a little different, Becky thought. So much had happened on the ride. The proud princess seemed a little messier, her white track suit soiled, the tensor bandage around her ankle not exactly a fashion statement, her hair mussed. There was a softer look to her face as she stood smiling at her.

"Good luck on your Arabian race," Becky said. "You and Hawk. Let us know how you do."

"Of course I will. Good luck to you, and Rob." Tara's mouth twitched into a smile. "He's a great guy."

CHAPTER 22

LEAVING THE MOUNTAIN

It had been a week since the Wildflower 50.

Time had crawled by. Without Rob to do the ranch work, Becky had helped her father ride fences, repair one of the barns and look after the horses. But through it all, Rob had filled her thoughts. She missed him so much, it hurt.

Becky felt guilty for focusing so intently on her own troubles. As soon as they had got back to Mustang Mountain, word came that her cousin Alison had been in a terrible barrel racing accident that weekend. She was going to be okay, but she was still in the hospital. Becky knew she should be worrying about Alison, but all she could think about was a whole winter without seeing Rob.

She could remember every detail of their last moments together, before Rob left for Horner Creek.

The morning after the race, Rob had been saying goodbye to Shadow. He stood, petting the little paint, and she'd nuzzled his shoulder—as if she knew she was Rob's favorite.

"She likes you," Becky laughed, stepping out of the trailer. "Even if you are too tall to ride her."

"I think she does." Rob gave Becky his special grin. "I hope she's not the only female with a soft spot for me."

"You mean Tara? She sure had her eye on you."

"Don't start that again!" Rob burst out before he saw the teasing grin on Becky's face. "You never had to worry about Tara." His voice grew husky. "There was only one girl in the Wildflower 50 I wanted … still want."

"Rob!" Becky threw her arms around him. "I can't stand it that you're leaving."

Rob brushed a stray curl off her forehead and bent to kiss it. "Don't worry," he said softly. "Time will go fast. I'll be in school and running the ranch. You'll be helping your folks at Mustang Mountain. Maybe next summer—"

He broke off.

Becky felt as though her heart might break. Next summer might as well be forever.

But six weeks later, Becky found herself hurtling down the highway in the Mustang Mountain truck with her mom and dad. It was all because of Alison, amazingly enough. She was doing so well that her family and friends were throwing a surprise party for her sixteenth birthday that night.

Becky was looking forward to seeing Alison, but she was even more excited about tomorrow. Tomorrow, she would see Rob. Her heart sang. She wished the truck could zoom even faster down the wide highway.

The next morning, Becky was perched on a fence at the Kellys' Twin Rocks Ranch, watching Rob work with a palomino horse.

"How was the party?" he called to her, never taking his eyes off the horse, keeping his body turned away from its head.

"Fine," she called back. "It was fun."

She could remember clearly her first sight of Rob—so tall and so good-looking. She remembered the way he'd smiled at her, as if they were already friends. It had made her knees weak.

Becky still felt that way, seeing Rob in his jeans and cowboy hat, training a horse. She had news from last night, but she was nervous about telling him. Would Rob be glad to hear it? Had he changed his mind about her since he went back to school and the ranch and his old life? It had been almost two months.

Finally, Rob released the horse and strolled over to

the fence. He squinted at her from under the brim of his hat. "So the birthday party was fun. How's Alison doing?"

Becky grinned at him. "Alison's feeling better. She's ... different somehow since the accident. Nicer, maybe. She listens when you talk to her instead of going on and on about herself. She wanted to hear all about the Wildflower 50, and she asked about you ..."

"Glad to hear it." Rob was looking at her as though he never wanted to stop looking. "How long can you stay? When do you have to leave for Mustang Mountain?"

"That's the thing. Maybe I don't have to leave." Becky took a deep breath and launched into her news. "Alison asked me to come and live with her and Aunt Marion again."

Rob took off his hat. "So, do you think you could? Stay here and live with them? I guess it would be pretty tough."

"Well," Becky teased, "I put up with Tara during the Wildflower—she was a lot worse than Alison."

"That's for sure. And there'd be some good things about living with Alison." Rob counted them off on his fingers. "For one thing, you could go to school in Horner Creek. For another, you could keep Shadow here at the ranch, and we'd pick up her training where we left off. And ... you could maybe go out with me, sometimes." He was trying to keep it light, but underneath was a serious question, Becky knew.

She found herself blushing. "All of that would be good."

"What do your parents think?" Rob asked, looking into her face with that shy smile.

"They think I should move here," Becky nodded. "Dad says it's a shame to miss all the fun of high school, and Mom says her back is feeling better. There's not as much work on the ranch in the winter, anyway."

"So it's up to you." Rob shrugged. "If it works out, and you could stand living with Alison and her mom again, I'd like it, a lot."

"You would? Well, that's good—" Becky took a deep breath, "because I'm going to do it. I made up my mind last night."

She jumped off the fence into Rob's arms. They closed around her. Becky had waited a long time for this moment, but it had been worth the wait. It looked like she wasn't going to be so lonely this year, after all.

My name is Kathleen and I'm 13 years old. Just like you when you were a kid, I also love books and horses. Horses have been my favourite animal since I was very small. I love your Mustang Mountain series. I have numbers 1 to 6. Once I started reading them I couldn't put them down. I hope you continue to write more of these books. If you do, you can be sure that I'll be reading them.

My name is Courtney Hoffman. I'm a 13-year-old horse lover. I have my own horse. Her name is Cougar. She's a 10-year-old quarter horse mare. She's so much fun. Anyway I love your Mustang Mountain books! They're all so good. I've read books #1–6. I haven't received Mustang Mountain 7 yet, but I will. And I cannot wait until Mustang Mountain #8 comes out.

I read book three of the Mustang Mountain series. I love them. They're so good I think you're the greatest author in the world. I'm in grade five. I'm 10 years old. I really hope you write back to me because l love your books so much. —Sarah

Hi! My name is Stevie (my nickname). (My real name is Stephanie.) I'm in grade six. I love reading your Mustang Mountain series! When I read your books I feel like I'm actually there.

Sky Horse #1

Meg would do almost anything to get to Mustang Mountain Ranch, high in the Rocky Mountains. She wants a horse so badly. A sudden storm delays the trip and begins an adventure that takes Meg, her friend Alison and Alison's cousin Becky far off the beaten track. To reach Mustang Mountain, they'll need every scrap of courage they possess.

ISBN 1-55285-456-6

Fire Horse #2

Meg, Alison and Becky are alone at the Mustang Mountain Ranch. When two horses go missing, the girls and their friend Henry set out on a rescue mission. Caught in a forest fire, they save themselves and the missing horses with the help of a wild mustang stallion.

ISBN 1-55285-457-4

Night Horse #3

Returning to Mustang Mountain Ranch for the summer, Meg, Alison and Becky meet Windy, a beautiful mare about to give birth to her first foal. Meg learns a secret too: a bounty hunter has been hired to kill the wild horses in the area. When Windy escapes the ranch, the girls move to protect the mare and the wild horses they love.

ISBN 1-55285-363-2

Wild Horse #4

On vacation at a ranch in Wyoming, Meg, Alison and Becky have a chance to ride wild horses. Alison doesn't care to participate. Her mood threatens the vacation. She changes, however, when she discovers a sick wild horse. As hope for the sick horse fades, Alison must conquer her anger and come up with a plan to save it.

ISBN 1-55285-413-2

MUSTANG MOUNTAIN
Adventure awaits in the Rocky Mountains

Rodeo Horse

Sharon Siamon

Rodeo Horse #5

Alison and Becky prepare to join the competitions at the Calgary Stampede. Becky wants to find out more about Rob, the mysterious brother of a champion barrel racer. Meg meanwhile is stuck in New York, longing to join the Stampede. An accident threatens the girls' plans. Or was it an accident?

ISBN 1-55285-467-1

Brave Horse #6

A phantom horse, a missing friend, a dangerous valley filled
with abandoned mine shafts … Not exactly what Meg, Alison
and Becky were expecting on vacation at the Mustang Mountain
Ranch. Becky had expected a peaceful time without her annoy-
ing cousin Alison. Alison had expected to be traveling in Paris.
And Meg had planned to meet with Thomas. Instead, the girls
must organize a rescue. Will they be in time?

ISBN 1-55285-528-7

Free Horse #7

New adventure begins while Meg and Thomas care for a neighbouring lodge and its owner's rambunctious 10-year-old stepson, Tyler. The trouble starts when Tyler opens a gate and lets the ranch horses out. In his search, Thomas discovers that someone is catching and selling wild horses. Could it be Tyler's brother Brett and his friends? A hailstorm hits and Thomas fails to return to the lodge. Can Meg and Tyler find Thomas and save the wild horses?

ISBN 1-55285-608-9

Swift Horse #8

Alison Chant is angry at the world. She wants a new horse, but everything gets in her way. First, her mom says, "No more horses!" Then, she finds the horse of her dreams, but it belongs to a young girl named Kristy Jones, who refuses to sell her beloved Skipper. Finally, Alison takes matters into her own hands, only to get Skipper and herself into terrible trouble at a barrel race. Who can save her? Does she have the courage and strength to make things right?

ISBN 1-55285-659-3

WALRUS
B O O K S

AN IMPRINT OF WHITECAP BOOKS

ABOUT THE AUTHOR

As a child, Sharon Siamon was crazy about two things—books and horses.

Born in Saskatoon, Saskatchewan, Sharon grew up in a farming area of Ontario. She learned to ride by coaxing a farmer's big workhorses over to rail fences with apples, then climbing on their backs and riding bareback till they scraped her off under the hawthorn trees that grew along the fence. She wished for a horse of her own and read every horse book she could find.

Sharon has been writing books ever since for kids who dream of having adventures on horseback, among them *Gallop for Gold* and *A Horse for Josie Moon*. The Mustang Mountain adventures began with a wilderness horseback trip through the Rocky Mountains. Sharon's friends in the exciting fields of barrel racing and endurance riding have kept the adventure going. So far, the Mustang Mountain books have been translated into Norwegian, German, Finnish and Swedish.

Sharon writes back to all the fans who write to her at her email address: sharon@sharonsiamon.com.